Drinking Until Morning

Justin Grimbol

www.blackcoffeepress.net

Putting the "F" back in Fiction.

For Jay Gorcoff

There's no doubt about it,
Death's death. Once you see that, you'll
see that turning down drinks is for fools.

-T'ao Ch'ien

1

She was tall and had short curly brown hair and a flat chest. Her eyes were wide and filled with a silky sadness that made me feel I had three hearts: one in my chest, one in my dick, and one in her eyes somewhere, feeling dusty and abandoned.

I watched her as she got dressed. It was early. Sunlight came through the windows and lit the arch of her back as she put on her jeans.

"Stop looking at me like that," she said. "I don't want to sleep with you. I'm hungry and grumpy and the last thing I want to do is touch your little ding-dong. So stop bothering me."

I have known her for a long time. We met just after my mother had died and I was having anxiety attacks as frequent as a teenage boy gets an erection. Things were sweet between us back then. It never felt too bleak because here I was dating this young girl, Zoe Booblanaski, and she didn't seem to know how to do anything but make me happy. When we had sex she came over and over again. Most likely she was faking it, but I couldn't tell the difference. So, as far as I was concerned life was blissful.

Then she started drinking and acting cold towards

me. We fought constantly. I was like an abused housewife, constantly begging her not to go to the bars, then spending all night watching movies and crying and eating ice cream. When she got home I would be awake and waiting in her housecoat. The fighting would start up again. We would yell and throw things. She would then run off and keep drinking until morning. She'd return home only to wake me and ask if I could drive her to 7-Eleven to buy more beer.

Eventually I snapped and told her I didn't want to see her anymore.

A year or so passed.

In a moment of weakness, I decided to call her, see how she was doing. She told me that she had stopped drinking and that she missed me.

We started seeing each other again, usually meeting in motels since I had moved back home to Sag Harbor and now lived in the same house I had grown up in. My aunt Hilda, whom I called Aunty, was renting it from my father, who now lived with his new wife on Shelter Island, which was closer to the church he had been the minister of for the past ten years.

The house was exactly as it had been before my mother died. Aunty hadn't changed a thing. She kept it like a shrine. All the furniture was where she had left it. And with the house, Aunty had also taken on my mother's dogs: two Sharpeis named Harold and Maude.

The only noticeable difference in the house was that my old room was now being used for storage. So I moved into my parent's room. Again, everything was just how my mother had left it. There were still all these photos... of family, my parents' wedding and me as a child, hanging there in the dust.

Zoe felt uncomfortable having sex in my new room.

"I can't handle this," she told me.

"What's wrong?" I asked.

"I can't get myself off while looking at that crazy fucking picture!" she yelled.

Hanging above the bed was a large portrait of me that had been taken when I was three. In the picture my big head is covered by blonde hair and I am trying to cover my smile with my little hand. I still have a big head and tiny hands. My eyes are still pretty. It's just that the rest of me has grown large and sloppy. I now have a big beard and bruises on my chest from punching myself when I feel anxious. There are three huge pink stretch marks to the right of my belly button. But other than that, though, I figured I still looked about the same as I did in that picture, but just bigger.

"Who is that little boy?" she asked.

"It's me," I told her.

"That's so creepy."

"Just don't look at it."

My old home was not very conducive for love making. It wasn't just the pictures that made Zoe uncomfortable. There was also my aunt. I grabbed Zoe by the waist and laid her on her stomach. She had a muscular back. I kissed her shoulder blades and then down her spine to her ass, which was warm.

"Dustin! Dustin! Are you in there?" Aunty yelled.

Her voice sounded urgent. I thought maybe one of the dogs had been killed, maybe hit by a car or attacked by another animal.

There was a knock at the door. I pulled my face out of Zoe's ass crack.

"Hey Dustin! Dustin!"

"Yes!" I answered.

"I got your laundry."

"What?"

"I cleaned that sweatshirt you like to wear. You know, the one with the sleeves cut off."

Zoe got scared and hid herself under the blankets.

3

This meant that the sex was over. I knew how she worked. Her pussy was as neurotic as she was. It had a short attention span. Once I was out, it was hard to get back in. It couldn't handle distractions. It was like it had Attention Deficit Disorder. Sometimes I wanted to stick Ritalin in there just so it could focus.

"Dustin, honey, can I come in?"

"I said hold on!"

I got out of bed and opened the door. I was still naked, still sweaty, disheveled and hard.

She was a short, stocky woman. For more than twenty years she had been getting the same crew-cut. Many of my friends had figured that she was a Lesbian. But for as long as I'd known her she hadn't ever been with anyone. She was asexual.

"What do you want?" I asked.

Aunty smiled at me nervously and then handed me the sweatshirt. It was still warm from the dryer and it smelled clean.

"I'm sorry for bothering you," she said.

"It's fine," I told her, trying to be less agitated.

I watched her sulk down the hall.

When I closed the door Zoe poked her head out of the blankets.

"Is she gone?" she asked.

I nodded.

"That woman scares me," she said.

"I know."

"She doesn't like me."

"Probably not."

I got back into bed and tried to pick up where we had left off, but as I expected, she was unresponsive.

After four years of this, I still hadn't gotten used to it. She made me feel like a lost child in Wal-Mart.

4

Later that night I found Aunty in the kitchen. She was eating a milkshake. She liked to buy them from McDonalds, put them in the freezer for a couple of days, wait till it got all freezer burnt, then eat it like it was ice cream.

"Do you want one?" she asked. "I got a couple extra in the fridge."

"I would love one," I told her. "Thanks."

The texture of the milkshake was strange, almost crusty. After being in the freezer it became crunchy and almost seemed to enhance the flavor.

"This is delicious," I told her. "I think I might like this better than normal ice cream."

"Do you want the rest of mine?" she asked.

"Do you mind?"

"No, go ahead. I'm just glad you like it."

I tried to eat this one slowly. It was late. Neither of us could sleep. The dogs were outside barking. I looked out the window to see what had excited them. It was too dark, though, and I couldn't see anything.

"They miss your mother," Aunty said.

"I think they're just dogs," I told her. "They can't help themselves."

2

A couple of days later Zoe stopped letting me sleep with her. She said she just wasn't in the mood. This brutalized me. Why? Why wasn't she in the mood? Was it because I shaved my pubic hair off? I thought it would make my dick look bigger, but it hadn't. I was fat and fat men need pubic hair otherwise their privates look pudgy and awkward, like the ass of a pig. I had messed up. I wanted to be sexy.

I was disappointed in myself. I thought I could handle her, that I could withstand her coldness. And instead of groveling at her feet, begging her to love me, I would be stoic. I would show her such calm and wisdom that could only be compared to that of the Buddha or Christ. And it would make her pussy so wet that her heart would follow. I would melt this iceberg of a woman. Global warming had nothing on the sweet wisdom in my eyes. I would make this girl so wet the whole world would drown.

I thought had grown so much since the last time she left me. In my mind, what once had been a spoiled little boy was now hardened into a tragic hero, like Robocop.

But she was able to break me down so easily. My strength relied on the sweet, musky sloppiness of her pussy, lunatic scream in her eyes, and the kindness of her long arms. I relied on all of this the same way Popeye relied on his spinach. Without those things I was just flimsy. The only muscle that worked was my needy little penis that shyly hung in front of my huge balls.

It took all the energy I had to hold it together, to not break down and act like a complete sissy.

I had trouble sleeping. When I did I had dreams about my mother. In them the doctors had fixed her. She was alive again, but something was missing. Everyone else thought the doctors had made her better. She was taller, healthier. She acted more cheerful and less temperamental than she did before she died. People liked this. But I thought something was missing. I tried to convince everyone that she had gone insane. Look at her eyes, I would say. Look at them. They aren't like they used to be. See how she looks at me. They are not aching; they are not moist. It's like I'm not even her child.

When I woke up Zoe was facing me. I tried to wake her by kissing her cheeks and her forehead. She groaned, pushed me away and then turned over. Even in her sleep she was a bitch. I wanted to strangle her. I wanted us both to be awake and screaming.

Instead, I went to the bathroom and like I often did when Zoe wasn't looking, I wept. And as I did I stared at my naked body in the mirror. At least I still looked like a man. I had balls. I had huge balls. And I had a beard; although it was long, it was also thin and transparent in spots. Most of all, it was silly, but then again so was my heart.

3

"I think I'm going to move to Florida," Zoe told me, "and live with my mother."

We were eating bagels at the Wharf in downtown Sag Harbor.

"When are you going to do that?" I asked.

"Soon," she said. "I hope I can move as soon as possible."

I didn't want her to leave, but I didn't tell her that. I pretended to be excited for her. I told her I thought I could imagine her being happy there, that I could see her walking on the white sands, resting under palm trees and playing with little lizards. She liked this. It made her happy to think about Florida. It still had that new car smell in her mind.

And apparently, thinking about Florida also made her horny because when we got back to my room we kissed and wrestled and giggled like children. She let me fuck her again. She got on all fours with her ass spread open, her anus winced at me. I bent down, sniffed and licked her till her pussy was wet.

I put it in.

It felt good in there. Each thrust, each stab I took was a prayer. I had found my Mecca. Thank you, I prayed, moaning louder than a dog stuck in a kennel. Thank you, oh God, thank you! I was a prophet waving his cane at God, then striking it into the ground. The earth shook. It sang to me the way the ocean sings to the sand. It told me that I was the best fucking lover the world had ever known because I was strong, because I was durable, because I loved my dead mother, because I stayed up night after night eating my own boogers. I was the best lover the world had ever seen because I cry so easily. By doing everything wrong I had done everything right. Her body told me that. Being such a sissy I had become as rugged as a cowboy. Ride on, it said to me. Ride on Grimboli, ride on into the sunset.

4

Zoe moved to Florida a couple weeks later. The transition was difficult for her and she called me frequently. That was a lonely, but peaceful time. I missed Zoe, yet I found her constant phone calls reassuring. I knew the affection was temporary, but I embraced it as if it was something as reliable as the love of a dog.

When we weren't talking I spent my time working on my collages. I was combining images from porn magazines with images from old video games. Rarely had I enjoyed creating art as much as I enjoyed making those collages. The images came together so easily.

Some of the pieces I made were abstract. In one I put a digital mushroom over an out of focus breast. Others were made simply for shits and giggles. I would take a picture of Link, the hero from the game *A Legend of Zelda*, and replace his sword with a picture of a cock.

Aunty would come home from work at around eight or nine at night. I would hear her car pull into the driveway and then quickly put away the porn mags. One night I had passed out in the living room, though, and she had found the magazines. She didn't act upset. All she had done was stack them neatly in the corner of the kitchen.

Still, I felt guilty. And this guilt changed how I viewed my art. The collages looked strange to me now. They didn't seem artistic anymore. They looked liked something a crazed pervert would create, like a statue made out of little girl panties.

The last time I felt that guilty about something I had created was when I was ten. I had drawn a comic about Freddy Krueger. It was called *Nightmare on Elm Street Infinity*. In it Freddy fucks a girl with a penis shaped like a chainsaw. My mother had found the comic and lectured me for hours about how I was exploiting women. I was young and had no idea about what she was talking about. Still, I felt horrible. The way she looked at me filled me with shame.

That night I burned the comic. The printer paper it was drawn on lit up into a bright flame. And as I watched it sizzle into ashes, I was sure that I had purified myself.

It felt that much worse to be creating such art so many years later. Back then I could say I was just a kid, that I didn't know any better. At age twenty two it was not so easy to rationalize this kind of behavior.

Maybe it was all in my head. Maybe the art was not as perverted as I thought. Maybe, just maybe, even the old Freddy Krueger rape-comic was actually a work of genius and it was actually my mother who was in the wrong.

It became clear to me that my work had to be viewed by the public. *Nightmare on Elm Street Infinity* got sent to the flames without any audience other than my overly emotional mother. It wasn't right. My video game porn needed to be given the chance to be seen.

The first person I told about the porn-art was Zoe. She didn't seem to think they were all that perverted, but she didn't think they were very creative either.

"They just sound kinda dweeby," she said.

This made me feel worse. It would have been better if

she would have been offended. It would have made me feel guilty, but still, I would have actually affected her in some way. I couldn't stand how crushingly apathetic her voice sounded.

In order to provoke her I started talking in more detail about all the porn-art I had been doing, hoping that one of the pieces would disturb her in some way.

"Oh yeah, that one seems real interesting," she kept saying. But she sounded bored. It was clear that she was only letting me go on like this out of pity.

I described each collage until finally, one got to her.

"It's my favorite," I told her. "I got Mario and Luigi's heads both sticking out of this fat lady's pussy, making it so it looks like she is giving birth to both of them at the same time."

There was a long awkward pause.

"What's wrong?" I asked. "Why aren't you talking?"

"That last painting you told me about..."

"It's a collage."

"Yeah, well, whatever it is, something about it really freaked me out. I don't know."

"I'm sorry," I said.

"It's ok... I mean, you didn't do anything, really."

I pretended to be apologetic, but on the inside I felt triumphant. Finally! I had gotten to the bitch! My heart was the beating applause of a thousand men! It was like I was on a hill and all I had to do was show them my sweaty, little penis and they were all applauding. Even the Tin Man from the *Wizard of Oz* was there, because I had given him something even better than a heart. I had given him his dick back.

I had truly offended Zoe. Knowing this, I slept soundly. My dreams were full of shame, but it was still a deep sleep and when I woke up the next afternoon, I felt rested and ready to take on the day.

5

Zoe started calling me less and less and when she did call it was obvious that it was just to hear a voice.

I needed to get down there. Once I was with her I could reignite something between us. This strategy had never worked in the past. Most times, when I had hunted her down, it had only made her act more repulsed by me. Still, I felt it was what I needed to do.

To make the trip a little easier to handle, I decided to invite my buddy Kalish. He was a tall, dark, hardworking Italian and the only way to get him away from his work was the idea of a real vacation, in the most traditionally American sense of the word. There needed to be cozy, air conditioned hotels, beaches and lots of souvenirs to bring back to his family. He liked to be a tourist and he felt absolutely no shame in it. His goal was to recreate the type of vacations his mom and dad had taken him on when he was a kid. For him, Florida was the perfect vacation spot. What he couldn't understand was why I wanted to go to there.

When I told him that Zoe lived down there he became concerned.

"Jesus, Grimboli, you're going to have me drive all the way down to Florida so you can do what, get laid once, fight and then cry the rest of the time?"

"Relax Kalish, I promise we will only stay at Zoe's for a couple of days; whatever sex and fighting and crying goes on, will be condensed into a very small portion of the trip. The rest of the time will be filled with everything your little wop heart desires. Besides you will like Zoe's place. Her mom's filthy rich. It will probably be better than any hotel we can afford."

"Did you just call me a wop?"

"Yes, it's a derogatory term for Italians and..."

"Grimboli, I know what the word means."

There was silence. The tension between us could get thick.

"So are you coming or not? It's no big deal to me. I can do it alone if I have to."

"You are going to drive all the way down to Florida alone?"

"Sure, why not? It's no big deal."

Truth was, I was terrified to go alone and he knew it.

"I'll go," he said. "But you better promise your goddamn girl drama better not get in the way of my vacation."

"I promise."

"Fine."

"Hey Kalish..."

"What?"

"I love you."

"I love you too Grimboli..."

6

My sleeping patterns were fucked. Most nights I went to bed as late as five or six in the morning, then I would end up sleeping until late the next afternoon. My sense of time was completely skewed. The afternoon felt like morning and nighttime felt more like the afternoon. And just when I was feeling tired the sun would be coming up and the birds would begin to chirp. So I decided to start the trip to Florida in the middle of the night.   We drove straight through. By the time the sun was rising I still had plenty of energy left in me. Kalish, on the other hand, looked exhausted. Strangely, he was the one who demanded that we drive without stopping for anything but gas and food. "We're got to power through," he kept saying.

The farther south we got the more billboards we saw. They were either advertizing for Bible outlets or porn shops. There also seemed to be about a thousand signs for a place called South of the Border. We stopped there and were surprised to find a rickety, side of the road store that sold only t-shirts for a dollar. We had no interest in buying any shirts, but we got out of the car anyway and stretched our limbs. The last time we had been out of the car it had been cold and damp with the looming threat of snow. Now it was so warm we had to change into t-shirts and shorts. We ran around the parking lot as if the sun shine was coming down like snowflakes. It was exciting. All we had done was go south, but it felt like we had invented fire.

7

Zoe lives in a rich, gated community in Naples. We arrived there at two in the morning and we were both deliriously tired. My mind felt as soft and sweet as a marshmallow. Luckily, Zoe was excited to see us. If she wasn't, I would have burst out crying right then and there.

She embraced me with those long arms. She grabbed me tight. She hung from my neck and kicked her legs like a little girl.

"Look at you," she said, patting my belly. "You've gotten so big."

"I've been eating lots of milkshakes," I told her.

"Your mom has an impressive set up," said Kalish.

"Oh, I know. It's like so tacky, but there's an indoor pool. You wanna see it?"

We walked inside and put down our bags. It was unreal. Her living room and pool were under the same roof. Half the room was covered in shag carpeting and leather sofas, while the other half was set up like a lagoon surrounded by palm trees and exotic flowers. There was a waterfall that poured over the rim of the hot tub.

Kalish started crawling around the rocky ledges of the pool, pretending like he was some sort of cave creature. He was tall and gangly. His face was small and bird-like with a massive Adam's apple. Watching him move like that was hysterical.

"Oh my God, your friend is so funny," Zoe told me.

"I know," I said.

His comedy got me excited. I decided to strip down right where I was standing. Kalish started laughing as soon as he saw that I was naked. I shook my body and gave them a little show and then jumped in the pool.

"What the hell is going on?" Zoe yelled. "You guys are acting crazy. Are you drunk or something?"

"No," I said. "We're just tired."

Eventually Kalish went to bed, leaving Zoe and I alone swimming. We swam around silently staring at each other. There were thousands of insects outside making all kinds of god awful noises. I could feel them watching us.

Zoe dipped her mouth under the water and made bubbles. I swam over to her but she dodged my kiss. I couldn't understand what was wrong. All I wanted to do was kiss her then take her to bed. It had been a long drive, the longest I had ever driven. My mind was like a Jenga tower. It was teetering back and forth. One false move and it would fall.

"Listen Zoe," I said. "I'm too tired for games. Am I sleeping in your room or the guest room with Kalish?"

She looked angry and hurt.

"Then let's go to bed," she said.

I followed her to her room.

Her bed was large and her blankets and pillows were so fluffy that I could have gotten lost in them.

I tried to kiss her. Again, she denied me.

"Zoe, what the fuck is going on?"

"I just wanted us to lie here and cuddle first," she said.

"I'm sorry," I told her.

"It's fine," she said. "Just a little disappointing."

I started kissing her. She was more submissive than

passionate. When I climbed on top, her pussy was very dry.

"Spit on it a little," she told me.

I spit on my hand, rubbed her and then wiggled myself in.

Having sex was difficult. Her bed was set up in a way that made it difficult to move. The legs of the bed had wheels and they rested on platforms which raised the bed an extra three inches off the ground. Even the slightest movement made me feel like the bed was about to fall over.

"I'm scared of the bed," I told her.

"Do you want me to just suck you off and then we can just go to sleep?"

"Is that ok? I'm really tired."

My voice sounded as pitiful as I felt. I didn't deserve a woman to touch me in this way. I deserved a punch in the face. If only it wasn't for that crazed bed. I would have given her all I had. It would have been the storm of the century. I would have filled her with heat lighting. I would have fucked her so hard that her mother would have come in her sleep. Instead I was just lying there, begging for a blow like a fucking thirteen year old.

And she gave me some of the best head I had ever had. As far as I was concerned it was the best anyone had ever had, ever. I came quickly.
It oozed out like lava.

"That tasted horrible," she said. "That tasted like ear wax."

"But you like it 'cause you love me."

"Whatever."

I was so deliriously tired that I thought she was being affectionate. No matter what she said, all I could hear was the softness of her bed and the smooth emptiness of my recently drained penis.

She watched me as I drifted into sleep and when I woke up I was alone.

8

Zoe's mom was terrifying. She was more than six feet tall. Her breasts were massive. Just looking at them made me feel like I was about to get knocked over. She was a very haggard and worn-out looking woman. Her eyes were sunken and her tanned skin was rough and sad. Still, she was undeniably sexy. Kalish commented on her immediately. "She gives out the impression that you can fuck her," he said. "Which is strange because she is a mom."

Usually when one of my girlfriend's mothers met Kalish, I can tell they wish their daughter were dating him instead of me. But with Zoe's mother, Hillary, it was different. It didn't seem like she wanted Zoe to be with Kalish at all. She wanted Kalish for herself.

She liked to watch him. When he talked he flailed his arms around wildly. I always found that Kalish's gestures would be perfect for comedy. It was goofy to me. Hilary wasn't hearing anything funny though. As Kalish talked, she looked like she was listening to soft jazz.

This flirtation between them worked out to my advantage. With Kalish there I didn't have to engage in any small talk. I didn't have to talk at all. Kalish could monologue for hours. Hilary would take us all out to lunch and dinner and I would just eat and watch him entertain.

That night I tried to sleep with Zoe again, but she pushed me off of her.

"I'm just not feeling very sexy," she said.

I started crying.

"What's wrong?" she asked.

I didn't answer.

She tried to be sweet. She kissed the back of my neck. I tried to mount her, but again, she resisted.

I continued crying.

Once I ran out of tears she became stiff and withdrawn. We started fighting. Our fighting was loud and we were nervous about waking up Kalish and her mother, so we went outside and we walked up and down the ink-black streets of her gated neighborhood. We fought out all of our old fights. She was too cold. I was too needy. It all felt stupid. She said she didn't want to be with me anymore. I agreed. As we yelled at each other little dogs woke up and started barking at us. It went on like this till dawn.

When we got home Kalish and Hilary were eating breakfast. They both looked at us and giggled.

"Well, it looks like you two had quite a night," Hilary commented, taking a sip of orange juice.

"Did you guys sleep on the beach?" Kalish asked.

"No," I said. "I spent the whole night crying and yelling at her."

"Really?"

"Yes, we fought all night."

"Should I grab my things?"

I nodded. Kalish could tell that I was going to cry again, so he rushed off and packed as quickly as possible. I spent the rest of the day sleeping in the car as he drove.

9

Kalish decided that in order to have the full Florida experience, we needed to head down to Key West.

We planned on staying a week, but as soon as we got there and discovered how expensive it was, we knew that wasn't possible. Our hotel room was the size of walk-in closet and it put us back a couple of hundred bucks a night. We couldn't afford to spend more than a night in this place.

Since the Keys are known for its night life, we expected to see something out of *Girls Gone Wild*. It was supposed to be Sodom and Gomorra but with palm trees. We had timed the trip poorly though. It was a Monday and the only club we found open was practically empty. A few men sat at the bar looking sullen. The place felt more like the waiting room in a hospital than a night club. I was the only person dancing. Kalish tried to dance but he felt too self conscious. Instead he just watched me and cheered me on as I danced alone.

After that we went to Duvall Street, where we found a strip club called the Devil's Slipper.

Kalish was shocked by my behavior. He had expected me to act more rowdy in a place filled with naked women, but I was more like a shy little boy. I got nervous like kids do when they have to sit on Santa Claus's lap in the mall and tell him what they want for Christmas.

There was one stripper that both of us were drawn to. Most of my life I had focused my attention on moody, dark haired women, but now I found myself loving blondes. This lady was very blonde and she had the longest legs I had ever seen. As she gave me a lap dance she got so close I could see all of her gooseflesh and little hairs. I was enchanted by her. I paid for lap dance after lap dance. With each dance she got more and more intimate. She would rub her face against my crotch. She would stand over me, spreading her ass open and then putting it in front of my face. She would nibble on my ear. It was wonderful. My heart was filled with slow, sexy explosions and my eyes were in flames.

At one point I gave her another twenty dollars to seduce Kalish. She walked over and sat on his lap. I watched them flirt. Their conversation looked like it was becoming serious. I got bored and walked away.

An hour later I saw her.

"Your friend is a very serious man."

"I know."

"He seems very driven."

"Did you give him a lap dance?"

"No," she said. "All he would do is talk about his job. He made me feel anxious."

"I'm sorry."

"Don't be. He is very handsome. I kinda enjoyed it."

Kalish went back to the hotel, but I stayed out and continued drinking and visiting the strip clubs. When I finally got back to the hotel room it was eight in the morning and I had spent most of my money. Kalish had just woken up. He wanted to get an early start on the day.

The only place that wasn't too expensive was the

aquarium. It wasn't very big. We roamed around the place slowly, studying all the strange, sleepy looking creatures. In the back there were sharks. Watching them made me dizzy. All they could do in there was swim in circles. I had an intense urge to throw something in the tank. It could be anything. It could be my wallet, a quarter, a pen, my camera. It didn't matter. I just wanted to make contact with one of those monsters in some way. The urge passed; I told Kalish I wanted to leave.

We spent the rest of the day driving up to Miami. He was determined to get a beach side hotel. I told him I didn't think it was worth it, that it would be too expensive. He got mad and started yelling at me.

"Have you ever stayed in a beach side hotel?"

"No, I haven't," I said.

"Well, then how the hell do you know if it's worth it or not?"

Kalish paid for the hotel.

It was a lonely place. I walked up and down the halls and saw no one but the woman who worked the front desk. I went for a walk to find a place to buy a soda or maybe a bar to drink a beer, but I found nothing.

The news said there was a cold front passing through. We hoped that it was an exaggeration. How bad could a "cold front" in Florida really be? We figured at worst the temperature would drop to eighty and in the morning we rushed out of the hotel in our bathing suits, hoping to have a fun day at the beach.

There was no fun to be had. The wind was blowing the sand at us so hard that it stung my skin. There was no one on the beach but us and a man who was holding his son. The poor little boy was sobbing as he tried to rub the sand out of his eyes. This was not the Miami I had seen on TV. There were no women in thongs sun bathing, there were no oily muscle bound men. It was just us, this father and his little boy pushing their way through a wasteland. It was horrible.

After Kalish did a little shopping, we decided to head home. We tried to drive straight, but I just didn't have it in me. I was exhausted. We made it to Georgia and then rented a room at a cheap motel.

There were two small beds in the room. Once we turned the lights out it felt like we were at Sleep-Away Camp.

"Isn't this fun?" I said.

"Sure," he said. "I guess it isn't horrible."

"It's been a real adventure. Even the shit with Zoe. It's all part of one big adventure."

"Really? It all seemed more sad than fun."

"Of course. I got my heart shat on, but fuck it. You've got to break a few eggs to make an omelet, right?"

"I'm glad you have been able to put such a positive spin on things."

"Me too," I said. "You know what? I think I finally got what it takes to get over this girl."

"Yeah, and what's that?"

"I don't know, but I sure got it!"

That night I woke up sweating and crying. I missed Zoe and it was hot. The room felt like a sauna. While still crying, I stumbled around in the dark until I could find the air conditioner. I played with the buttons until I felt cool air coming out of it. It felt good. I washed my face in the frosty blast of the AC and then made my way back to bed. The temperature in the room dropped quickly. The room now felt more like a meat locker. I had to go to the car and grab an extra blanket in order to keep warm.

I slept very well that night. It was so cozy under all those blankets that my mind didn't reach out for sad dreams about Zoe.

When I woke up in the morning, I saw Kalish lying in a fetal position, shivering violently.

"It's fucking freezing in here," he said. "I barely slept last night. I was so cold. I think we should ask for our money back."

I couldn't let him go to the front office and complain, then watch his embarrassment as they explained to him that the air conditioning was on too high. I had to confess.

"Listen Kalish," I said. "I got to fess up. I think I turned the air conditioning on last night..."

"You 'think' you might have turned on the air conditioning?"

I nodded nervously. Kalish inspected the air conditioner and played with it till it was off.

"I'm really upset," he said.

"I'm sorry."

Kalish looked over at me like he wanted to hit me. His patience was dwindling. I had to be careful or he would snap. He would yell at me and shake me and I would cry. It would all be so messy. I had to be very, very careful or we both would break.

It was a long drive home.

10

It was four in the afternoon and I was stumbling around the kitchen, in my dirty underwear, scratching and yawning. The Florida trip had left me feeling ruined. I missed the old anxiety women used to cause me. It was easier to deal with anxiety. All you had to do was get a little crazy and then you could convince yourself that what you were feeling was actually happiness. The anxiety was gone though and it had been replaced with a dimwitted sadness and all I wanted to do was sleep.

My aunt's car pulled into the driveway. Whenever she came home from work she would walk around the kitchen looking so tired and punished that even her eyes seemed to be slouching.

"Honey, what are you doing in your underpants?" Aunty asked while pulling out two milkshakes from the freezer.

"I just woke up," I told her.

I sat down and started eating one.

Aunty looked at me and smiled. It was almost as if she was proud of me.

"I don't know how you do it," she said.

"Do what?"

"I don't know how you sleep so much. The longest I

can sleep-in on one of my days off is till ten in the morning."

"I can barely remember what ten in the morning looks like anymore," I told her. "Is the sun closer to the earth at that time of day?"

She didn't get the joke. "No I don't think sun works that way," she said.

"I was just joking around."

"Oh Dustin, you are such a silly nilly."

"Where are the dogs?" she asked.

"They're outside."

"Oh no! Dustin! It's cold outside! They're probably freezing to death out there!"

"Aunty, they're dogs, they don't get cold like people do. They're made out of fur."

"Well, I know... but... still..."

Aunty rushed off and opened the back door. The dogs came scampering in.

"Oh, you poor things... did Dustin leave you out side in the cold?"

I looked over and saw Aunty sitting on the ground. She was letting the dogs lick her face. It made me angry. Something about the way the dogs were acting made me feel betrayed, like their excitement was their way of confirming with Aunty that I had, in fact, mistreated them.

Aunty and the dogs came into the kitchen. They were wet. It had been raining.

"So what are your plans for the evening?" Aunty asked.

"Research," I told her.

"Oh really! What kind of research?"

"It's complicated," I said.

This wasn't true. The research I was doing was not complicated at all. It wasn't even research really. All I did was stay up watching re-runs of old sit-coms. Mainly, I watched *Rosanne*. She was fat and loud and reminded me of my mother. I watched *The Cosby Show* and *Cheers* and all that, but the only show that actually got to me was *Roseanne*. As far as I was concerned, it starred my dead mother.

When someone talked badly about the show I took it as if they were talking about my mom.

That night I got a call from Zoe while I was "researching." I was thrilled that she called. After our fight in Florida I figured it would take her months to want to talk to me again.

"What are you doing?" she asked.

"I'm watching Roseanne."

"Ew," she said. "I fucking hate that show."

"Why?"

"Rosanne's a bitch. She's just so gross and loud and annoying. I have no idea how she got so famous..."

"She's reminds me of my mother," I said.

"Who reminds you of your mother?"

"Roseanne."

"Well, I'm sorry to hear that."

I didn't know what to say. I wanted to hang up on her, but I had been waiting for weeks for her to call me. I knew that if I hung up she would get mad and then it would take even longer for her to forgive me. So I kept on the phone, but I didn't talk much. I didn't have it in me.

11

My mother was a Presbyterian minister. The thing she was most successful with in her ministry was her youth group. She didn't attract the usual kids that go to youth groups. There were no real do-gooder types, no angels. Instead she attracted misfits , fuck-ups and nerds; It wasn't the smart type of nerd, but the type that smelled bad and chewed their nails until their fingers bled.

Her favorite members of the group were a pack of kids called the Rugrats. When I was in ninth grade they were the only kids left who hadn't reached puberty yet. They got their name from the cartoon which featured small, adorable looking trouble makers. At one point they tried to change their cliques name to TLP, which stood for True Little Players. But people didn't like the idea of them being "playaz" or them being sexy at all, or even sexual. They were too little. No, they were the Rugrats. This made them angry at first, but eventually they learned to not only to accept the name, but to embrace it.

It was hard to deal with them. They liked to take the usual mischief and bring it to a level that was uncomfortable for most other kids. We'd all be playing ring-and-run and then one of them would throw a brick through a cop car window. Still, no matter how much shit they got in, they came across as nothing more than rascals, not the criminals they wanted to be viewed as.

My mother thought they were adorable. It was bizarre to see them with her. She would hug them hard, pulling them into her fat arms like they were puppies. I never knew what it was she saw in them. There was no reason why she should have loved them so much. They were sleazy kids, thugs and future license plate makers.

Sometimes I would try to persuade her to see them as everyone else saw them.

"You should see them around girls," I would say. "It's horrible. I don't know why you feel the need to take care of them so much. They're pricks."

And she always replied the same way. "Compassion without reason, Dustin. That is the kingdom of heaven."

I didn't like it when she got like this. The way she talked made her sound like a televangelist.

Not long after she died, Slim and Milz, two of the main members of the clique, we're expelled from high school. They had gone into school wacked out on mushrooms and then assaulted the principal with a vacuum cleaner. There was nothing about the event that necessarily had anything to do with my mother. Still, I liked to imagine it was some sort of tribute to her and even though there was nothing very sweet about it, I appreciated it fully.

I started looking at them very differently. Their antics were no longer just humorous to me, but had begun to seem strangely liberating. I could understand my mother's draw to them. I didn't know how the Kingdom of Heaven had anything to do with it, but it felt good to be close to these kids and I made it my objective to be friends with them.

They didn't call me often but when they did I responded enthusiastically, like I was old and senile and they were my grandkids, who had finally been forced to call.

31

And even though I knew they were brats and that they were rotten, I loved them because they had sweet little voices and they distracted me from my normal habits of constantly over-analyzing and crying about things like women and death and no death and my aunt. Since I felt a need for them, I kept myself blind to how abnormal and cruel they could be.

Jesse was their leader. He was a little man with spiked, gelled hair and shallow eyes. There was something that seemed evil about him, something in how he talked and how he looked at you, that made it easy to imagine that if he was around during the second World War he would have been torturing Jews in Auschwitz. Still, there was a seductive quality to him as well' an intelligence that came through in his humor and his ability to turn the most wholesome night into something fully decadent. Slim and Milz were with him most of the time and they had the same type of personality, only not as intelligent and too sullen to be evil.

When they came over it was late, a little after midnight. I was standing in the bathroom looking at my body in the mirror. The three stretch marks on my gut made me look like I had been attacked by a cougar.

It made me feel good to see them. I hadn't seen anyone, but Aunty in weeks. Living with her was becoming difficult. She slept on the couch, not in her room. Maneuvering around the house without waking her was not easy. I had to have Jesse, Slim and Milz join me in the garage. That way it would be difficult for her to hear us.

Jesse sat on a dilapidated La-Z-Boy while Slim and I sat on the riding lawn mower. Milz just stood there, looking surly in his muscle shirt and his kitty-cat eyes. He rolled the blunt slowly. We all waited.

"I heard there's a party at Murph's house," Jesse said.

"There's supposed to be strippers," Milz added.

Slim got upset. "There's going to be nothing but dads

there. Fuck spending money on that shit. If I had bought some strippers I would just tell them to get naked and hang out and then, once I was a wild drunk, I would throw tomatoes at them."

"I wouldn't even spend money on that," Milz said.

"I like going to strip clubs," I told them.

"You should just watch porn," Jesse said.

"No, no, it's not the same. What I like is the smell and I like when I can see their goose bumps."

"Classic Grimboli," Jesse said. "Paying a bitch to see her goose bumps---who even does that?"

Milz finished the blunt. We smoked. Jesse started rambling wild things, non-sense things. We all laughed like crazed monkeys.

Everything Jesse said was pronounced like he was an umpire. "Look at the seagulls. Look at Grimboli look at the seagull's goose bumps. Grimboli loves the goose bumps. Grimboli loves the gooses. Grimboli loves bean and cheese burritos from 7-Eleven. Who the hell is that at 7's? It's Poetry Man reading poetry to a seagull."

We all laughed hysterically. We were sure what we were hearing was comedic genius.

"Holy shit! Holy shit!" he continued. "We need to go to 7-Eleven and find fucking Poetry Man."

I didn't know who he was talking about. I was too stoned to understand what poetry was let alone a Poetry Man. The only thing I could think of was Walt Whitman and his silly white poetry-beard. All I could imagine was him naked by the fire, masturbating while reading his own poetry. But that was not what they were referring to. They insisted Poetry Man was a living person who spent his time at our local 7-Eleven. Milz even recited one of his poems to me:

"A little boy sees a spider on a web. / It is a big spider. / It is an old spider. / It is a poor spider. / What's the boy going to do / shoot him with his bazooka?"

Jesse and Slim cackled like hyena's...

We drove to 7-Eleven, but he wasn't there. That was fine. I didn't actually believe he existed. Afterwards we drove to Heavens Beach. No Poetry Man. No poetry. Just a barren, humid, summer-night air like the ghost of a pussy. There were no waves at the beach. It was a just a massive puddle.

Eventually we gave up and Jesse called up a girl. She only lived a couple blocks from the beach. We walked to her house and then sneaked into her basement, so as to not wake the parents. She was fourteen, tall, Jewish, with curly black hair and marshmallow skin. She wore a black dress that was short and so light the fabric barely seemed affected by gravity. Slim and Milz were bored with her, but Jesse and I were completely hypnotized.

"Spin around," Jesse told her.

"Fuck you," she said. "You spin around."

We were cozy. The basement was furnished with leather couches and she brought down some of her parent's beer. Jesse kept insisting that she give us a show. She resisted, but Jesse was persistent and eventually she gave in. She spun her body around and her skirt lifted above her firm belly. Steady glimpses of ass and shaved pussy came at us with strobe light clarity.

"Oh man, oh man!" Jesse went on. "This is wild. Grimboli, you love this. You fucking love this. Don't deny it, you fat fuck. I show you the wildest shit."

"I'd rather look at a plant," Slim commented.

There was a brief pause and then Jesse started laughing.

I sat there nervously.

"What did you say?" the girl asked.

"I said I'd rather look at rutabaga?" he said.

Jesse, at his point, was on the ground hysterical.

34

"What the fuck did you say?" she continued.

Jesse got up off the floor and immediately became straight faced.

"He said fuck you, ya slut!"

The girl went wild. She started screaming at us, saying she was going to get her boyfriend to beat us. Jesse and Slim kept laughing. Milz was typing something into his cell phone.

Slim continued antagonizing her. "Your boyfriend is off getting drunk with strippers ya' turd, ya' smelly dweeb…"

She started throwing things---beer bottles, a lamp, her shoes---we ran out of the house, down the road, got in my car and then drove away. I could just see the girl's father carrying a double barrel shot gun and aiming at the back of the car.

As I drove off, Jesse was kicking my dash board pretending he was fighting the girl.

"Take that, and that. You like it don't you? Take that!"

I decided to drive us back to 7-Eleven. I needed to calm down, eat some shitty micro-waved food and let it sit, deep in me, let it fester and fizzle, like hydrogen peroxide on a scraped knee.

The parking lot was almost completely deserted. There was one guy who was pacing back and forth nervously. He was oily looking with no hair and a crooked nose. As he walked he caressed his cheeks. A delivery truck pulled up and he stared at it like it was Moses' burning bush.

"Look at that guy," I said. "He looks like eight hells and a bag a shit."

Jesse looked at the man and then proceeded to bounce up and down like a child.

"Oh shit! Oh shit! Yo Slim, it's fucking Poetry Man!" Jesse yelled.

We all rushed out the car.

I couldn't believe it. He was fucking real.

Jesse introduced me and he shook my hand

affectionately.

We chatted briefly about the weather and then he started reciting poetry to us.

> "a little boy sees
> a spider
> on a web. It
> is a big spider. It is
> an old spider. It is
> a poor spider.
> What's the boy going to do,
> shoot him
> with his bazooka?"

I was amazed. It was exactly what Milz had recited earlier.

"Do you want to hear another poem?" he asked.

I nodded.

"Well, it's based on a woman I knew," he said. "And every day I would see her she would say hi to me / and it made me feel very happy / to have such a tall pretty red head do that / and then one day she got married / and then she told me to keep away from her because I had touched her midriff / and I said fine / and I respected her because its feels nice enough / just to have someone that pretty / say hi once / let alone a whole bunch of times/ like she did---and that's the poem."

"Holy shit," Jesse said. "Holy shit. You hear that? That's the poem. Oh man, that is fucking nuts. That is fucking wild."

"Well, I got to go," he said. "You boys be nice to each other and don't sleep too much, you hear me?"

We all nodded.

He said good bye to us and walked away. He seemed to still be reciting poetry to himself, something about a rock.

"Milz, how many times have you heard him recite that poem about the bazooka?" I asked.

"Just once," he said. "Why?"

"How did you memorize it so exactly?"

He responded, sounding angry. "Same way I memorize every license plate number I see," he told me.

"You can do that?"

He nodded.

I rushed home after that, knowing that I was going to be able to sleep easily. Poetry Man dissolved in me like a sleeping pill. I dropped Jesse, Slim and Milz off and then all I needed to do was make it to my bed without waking my aunt.

Doing that was never easy.

"Dustin, is that you?"

"Yes Aunty. Go back to sleep."

"You woke me."

"I know; I'm sorry."

"It's ok."

I made my way to my bed and lie there a while staring at the shapes in the fake wood paneling that lined my parent's bedroom walls. It felt good to just lie there. Though I could have slept instantly, I decided it would be best to savor the exhaustion.

12

My dreams were emotional. They felt like my chest, my lungs and my eyes did when I tried to hold in tears after watching a sappy movie. Only in the dreams it's not my body that feels this way, but my home and the sky and the sound of the water or the eyes of some monster. That night, after listening to Poetry Man, I dreamt about the ferry I had to take to get from Sag Harbor to Shelter Island. There was a big barbecue on the ship and my mother was there. She was eating corn on the cob. That was it. There was nothing more in the dream, just the ferry, my mother and corn on the cob. Still something in all these things were trembling and when I woke up, I felt brutally hung-over. I pulled my blanket over my head to block out the sun.

One of the dogs started scratching on the door. I heard it push the door open. I told it to go away, but it didn't listen. It stood there whimpering. I turned over and faced the beast. It was Maude. She was weeping. Dragging behind her was a four foot long turd. She had eaten a sock and the fabric had interwoven throughout her feces.

"Aunty!" I yelled. "Help me!"

I hadn't yelled like that in a long time. When I was a kid I did this constantly. Whenever I lost something I would yell for an adult, usually my mother, for assistance.

"Dustin, honey, what's wrong?" Aunty hollered from the other end of the house.

"Just get over here! Quick! Hurry!"

She rushed over. She looked like she had just hiked a mountain. Her face was red and sweaty and her eyes were wild, almost rabid. She would do anything to protect me. She would lift a car or murder someone if she had to. Her eyes told me that.

"Dustin, what's wrong?"

I pointed at the turd. Maude was dragging it around my room leaving a trail of ooze in its wake.

Aunty seemed relieved.

"Oh, Maude's just a gotten into the sock drawer again." She proceeded to pull a plastic bag out of her pocket and then, using the bag as a glove, yanked the rest of the turd out the Maude's anus.

"It's a really long one this time," she said. "A tube sock. I'll go put it in the wash."

I was horrified. "Throw it away!" I yelled.

Where was I living? What is this place?

The dog, finally released from its shitty shackles, started running round the room.

"Well, look at her," Aunty said. "Maude's all full of piss and vinegar 'cause she just pooped."

She took the turd into the bathroom and flushed it down the toilet.

Maude also had a bad habit of eating plastic bags. When she shat them out they looked like jelly fish covered in tar. Aunty didn't act very concerned. It almost seemed like she thought it was cute. She would let Maudy go outside and watch her defecate.

"That's a girl," she would say, "just get the rest of it out. Geez, it looks like you ate the whole hamper this time."

Maude would come scampering back in and Aunty

would act proud of the beast.

Harold required less attention. He was calm. That was until Maude died. A couple of weeks after I saw Maude shit a sock, she died. The vet said from complications of having a hole in her stomach the size of a softball. Aunty was devastated.

"I think she missed your mother," she told me one night when she had finally stopped weeping. "And she knew that if she died she would get to be with her again. That's fine. They loved each other very much and I'm sure they're happy. I'm just worried about Harold now. He's going to be so lonely."

"It's going to be alright," I told her. "We'll take care of him."

I took her in my arms and let her weep. Harold was outside. He was running around looking happy as can be.

13

Aunty became harder and harder to deal with. She was constantly moping and whining about the price of dog food and about how her new boss treats her unfairly. It was like living with Eeyore from *Winnie the Pooh*, only not nearly as adorable.

I found myself tuning her out. This is a rotten thing to do to a person, but I couldn't help it. Occasionally I would have to ask her to stop.

"I'm sorry," I would say, "but I am trying to read."

She would apologize, walk off into the bathroom and start weeping. I have never had something that sounded so soft grind on my nerves so badly. It was horrible. It was like getting filled with dirt.

I got out of the house as much as possible and started to hang out with the Rugrats more and more frequently. We would go to a bar in Southampton called Willies.

I didn't fit in there very well. No matter how "fancy" I tried to dress I ended up looking like a dump truck. Women there didn't pay much attention to me.

There were these two girls, though. We had gotten bored one night and left early and we found them sitting on the hood of my car in the parking lot. From a distance they looked identical. They both had bleached blonde hair that went down to their shoulders and both wore pre-faded jeans and tight white shirts. As we got closer though, it became obvious that one was much younger than the other. They introduced themselves. The youngest called herself Mel-mel. She was our age, while Jerika, was in her early thirties.

We told them we would give them a ride, but we didn't have enough seats. Mel-Mel sat in the back, lying across Slim, Milz and my buddy Benedict's lap. Jerika sat in the front cuddling up with Jesse.

The ride was difficult. Jerika's voice was very loud, very distracting.

"I want cocaine!" she yelled. "I want fucking yayo! Don't any of you pussies have yayo?"

Milz snickered. "This bitch is fucking gross."

"What the fuck you say?" Jerika yelled.

Jesse tried to calm her.

"Relax baby, he's just flirting."

"Get your hand off my ass!" Jerika yelled.

"I have no idea what you are talking about," he said.

I looked over at them. Jerika's jeans were skin tight, but somehow Jesse had gotten his hands in there. He looked over at me and winked.

"Listen," Jesse went on. "I think we have a good situation here. You girls are cute. You obviously like to hook up and make out and maybe even touch our sling slongs. So why don't we cut the shit and go to your place and party?"

The girls laughed.

"Our roommates would hate you guys!" Jerika yelled.

"Why?" Benedict asked.

"Cause you all a bunch a pussies and our roommates are a bunch of big ol' black guys."

"Black guys love us," Jesse said.

Jerika told us that she didn't want to go home anyway. She wanted to go to a bar called Limbo, in Noyac.

As I drove on I heard Slim talking about the girl in the back seat.

"Benedict, what the hell are you doing?" he asked. "Make out with that. Look how bad she wants it. Fuck, if you don't do it I will."

I started hearing slurping noises, so I adjusted my rearview mirror to see what was going on. Benedict was an infamous prude. He was a good looking kid and dressed better than the rest of us, but he got weird around women. I was excited when I saw him in the back kissing this girl. It wasn't the most romantic moment though. Slim was fondling her breasts while Milz played with her pussy. You could tell that Slim and Milz weren't even getting off, that they were just trying to be rascals. Mel-Mel had no idea what was going on. She was too drunk.

From the outside the Limbo looked like the bars in Key West. It had a tacky, tropical motif. On the inside though, it was a regular dive bar. There was no one there but us, the bartender and some old guy that was nearly asleep on the counter. Benedict followed Mel-Mel around like a puppy dog. Occasionally she would give in and kiss him a little.

Slim and Milz had found Billy Joel on the juke box. I was surprised that they were such big fans of his music. They seemed like the type of guys that only listened to rap, maybe some R&B when no one was looking.

"I like Billy!" Slim kept yelling. "Billy is fucking rough! Listen to this kid. This shit is fully hood."

And then they started singing "Up Town Girl."

I sat at the bar watching everyone. They all seemed so precious right then, with Benedict all in love and the Rugrats singing Billy Joel. This is decent, I thought. This is a decent night.

While Benedict was in the bathroom Mel-Mel came over to me. We started flirting. The Rugrats had put on the song "We Didn't Start the Fire."

Mel-Mel leaned over and started kissing me. She then bit my lip. It hurt badly.

"I just bit you," she said.

I checked to see if I was bleeding. I kissed her again. It was soft this time, no biting.

"You bitch!" I heard Jesse yell.

I pulled away thinking he was talking to us, but he wasn't. He was going after Jerika, swinging his fists at her. She had scratched his face and he was now bleeding.

The guy that was asleep woke up and stumbled towards Jesse.

"This son of a bitch grabbed my titty Bruno; get him the fuck out of here!"

"You cunt!" Jesse yelled.

Mel-Mel hit me in the stomach and I doubled over.

"What did you do to my friend?" she yelled.

"I didn't do anything," I said.

She tried to kick me but I grabbed her foot and twisted it so she fell on the ground.

"You kids better get going," Bruno said to us, trying to be as diplomatic as possible.

"Obviously!" Slim said laughing. "This place is like that movie *From Dusk Till Dawn*! Shit seemed fully good here, then like in that movie you guys all turned out to be like crazed vampires or some shit."

I looked over at Jesse. He had gone crazy. He was growling and bent over and brushing his feet on the ground like a bull. This is what he used to do when we were young and would have fake wars on the play ground. Acting like a bull tended to disorient his opponent, making it a surprisingly affective fighting move.

"What the fuck is this little motherfucker doing?"

44

Bruno asked, looking confused.

Jesse charged, slamming his head into Bruno's crotch, knocking the juggernaut on the sticky bar floor.

"He killed Bruno!" I heard Mel-Mel mumble as she rolled around on the ground next to him.

Bruno slowly got to his feet. He threatened to beat us.

"You're going to beat us?" Slim yelled. "Fine, go for it! Fuck, I'll beat myself!"

Slim started punching himself in the face.

"Go ahead beat me. I don't even care."

"You're all crazy," moaned Bruno.

Things were getting too wild. I started trying to convince the Rugrats to leave.

"Jesse, I'm tired," I said. "I don't want to get beat up."

At first he was mad at me. "Grimboli, I'm mad about this," he said. "You're supposed to be on our side."

I found it adorable when he talked to me like this. Part of me wanted to keep fighting just to preserve a sense of companionship. Jesse could be very persuasive. He always made you feel like you were part of the team.

"I am on your side; I just want to leave," I told him.

"I'm mad at you Grimboli."

I heard the sound of a gun being cocked. It was the bartender. She had a shot gun.

"Get the fuck out!" she yelled at us.

We all ran out and got into the car. Everyone was quiet as I drove them home. Benedict looked like he was crying or maybe I just wanted to believe that. My soul felt chaffed and blistered. A little crying would have been soothing, like some sort of lotion.

14

Murphy started having strippers come and party at his house every other weekend. It became a very popular event in Sag Harbor. The Rugrats were the only people who didn't want to go. Benedict and I were curious though, so we decided to go without them.

I had expected the party to be much more wholesome than it ended up being. I imagined a regular party and that part way into the night a stripper would be brought in, hidden in a big cake or that maybe, they would show up at the door in costumes. My mind referenced movies more than it did things I had actually experienced and because of this I was frequently disappointed.

The party was in Murphy's basement. There wasn't much lighting. Electric camping lamps lit the area where the keg was and where the strippers were. There were six of them. They were separated into pairs and the guys gathered around them as they ate each other's pussies. Most of the men were older. Slim's dad was there kneeling near the strippers. His face was horribly pock marked and he seemed more interested in heckling the strippers than watching them.

"Come on!" he kept yelling. "You got to suck on that snatch! Yeah, yeah, you got to really suck on it! Jesus! I got to teach these girls how to eat a pussy, don't I?"

The rest of the men laughed.

I got bored. The dancing was an important element of the show. It's how a stripper shows her confidence. It's how she gets her power. These strippers didn't dance, they just ate pussy. They were compromised too quickly and the men were too big and loud.

Eventually the girls broke off and started walking around the room with buckets to collect tips. They were short and black and had chubby fish-like faces. When a guy gave them more than a dollar for a tip they let the guy spank them or suck on a nipple.

I saw another guy I knew there. His name was Dwight. He used to help my mother run her youth group. He was always stoned and had good stories. Physically, he was a shaved bear, but acted as gentle as a Newfoundland. We all loved Dwight. I almost went up and said hi to him, but he was intercepted by a stripper. Dwight gave her a ten dollar bill and she let him suck on her breasts. When he was done he looked around at his friend and laughed.

"Man, that girl got me horny as hell. My wife's going to get it tonight whether she wants it or not!"

Our eyes met, then drew away from each other in shame.

Benedict also seemed disturbed by things. He told me that the strippers had molested Murph's girlfriend and that she had run off crying. Murph's girlfriend, Natalia, was only sixteen, but she acted tough and it was unnerving to hear about her crying like that.

"I went to go look for her," he went on. "I found her in her car and man was she pissed. She was bitching on about Murphy and how mean he is and then when I told her she should leave him, she looked at me like I was crazy, she was all like talking this shit about how he loves her. 'You should see how he can be,' she kept saying. Fuck, she's out of

47

her mind, man."

"When people fall in love," I told him. "It's hard for them to imagine that the person they love doesn't love them back."

"I guess you're right..."

When I got home I found Aunty awake and eating a milkshake. I listened to her complain about her job and how much she missed Maude and how she felt bad for Harold. And, as usual, Harold seemed fine. He pranced around barking at the shadows and the dust that gathered there.

15

I woke up and thought it was early, but the sun was setting not rising. The light didn't have that violent, neon, blue in it. There were no bird noises. It was as if by waking up so late I had created a new clock and a new lonely dimension to live in. I could still see the old world. I could still see Aunty coming home from work and the dog running in circles in the back yard, but I saw it all through a sad, oily lens.

Everything seemed dirty. Maybe, I thought, everything was dirty. Dust danced on everything. My clothes reeked. I had been wearing the same outfit for weeks. They had probably smelled for a while, but it was only then that I was able to smell it. I undressed and started ransacking my room for something new to put on. Everything smelled like death. There were a few clean pairs of pants but they didn't fit me anymore. I had gotten bigger. I was fat as hell now. It was all those damn milkshakes, I thought. Aunty, that bitch; she was trying to get me fat.

I looked in the mirror. My stretch marks had gotten bigger. They were as red and as vibrant as the sunset.

I decided to walk into town. It was a short walk, just a mile or so. When I was a teenager I did this route frequently. In high school our gym teacher would have us walk a mile if we didn't want to participate in his activities. I was full of angst and rarely participated in anything. Somehow I convinced my principal to let me drop out of gym class and instead earn my gym credits by walking home from school. In my mind it was basically the same thing. Either way I was walking about a mile. The school agreed to my terms. My mother was very disturbed by how manipulative I could be. She thought that I was acting spoiled.

The first week of walking home was fun. I didn't regret my decision until the first day I had to walk through the rain.

I called my mother, asked her to come and pick me up, but she refused.

"You made your bed," she said. "Now lie in it."

It rained a lot that year. At times it seemed that every time I walked home it would rain. Even when it hailed she refused to pick me up. I would come home soaked and she would laugh at me and I would pout and run off to my room.

Now I could see the humor in it. Fuck... I would have done anything for it to rain that night. It seemed cleansing. Maybe it would wash the stretch marks off my gut.

But, instead of walking I decided to clean.

I went over my room dozens of times with the vacuum before I realized that the thing wasn't working.

"How long has this been broken?" I asked my aunt.

"Gee whiz Dustin, I don't know, I haven't been able to get that thing to work since I moved in here."

"This house hasn't been vacuumed since you moved in?"

"No, I don't think so."

After doing the dishes, I collected my clothing and brought them to the laundry room. The washing machine was filled with damp moldy bras and polo shirts. I asked my aunt if she could do something with her clothes so I could use the machine. The smell of mold was strong. It filled the laundry room and kitchen. Aunty waddled in and started transferring the wet clothes into the dryer.

"I'm sorry Dustin," she said to me.

"It's fine."

I started going through my clothes, looking for change. Aunty was in the kitchen. She was crying. I stood at the machine pretending to be sorting my laundry.

She finally stopped.

I heard the sound of leash being clipped onto a collar.

"Come on Harold," I heard her say. "Let's go. We got to find ourselves a new home."

I stood there and stayed as still as possible until they left.

It was ten thirty at night. Where was she going to find a place to live? It was absurd.

My mother used to complain about how passive aggressive Aunty could be. I always thought that she was overreacting, that my aunt was just sad.

I sat on the washing machine and felt it rumble under me and I thought about Aunty. Even when I was young I was aware of how sad she was. Every Christmas she would visit her mother in Ohio. She didn't like her mother so right after they finished their Christmas supper, she would rush back to Long Island to be with us. She would drive through the night and arrive at our house around dinner time the next day. Then we would have a second Christmas, something which, as a kid, I obviously loved. Still, I was also aware that something was off. As I would opened her presents she would be sitting there looking at me and she would be crying. Her crying scared me. So ,I would call for my parents, the way I had called to her when Maude was shitting out that sock. And they would come down to comfort her...

My mother was also sad, but in a way that was very different from Aunty. Both women had bad childhoods. Yet they had learned to deal with it in different ways. My mother carried her sadness like a huge deformity. It was like she had Elephantitis of the soul, and she didn't bother to get it amputated. She had learned how to carry it, to lug and maneuver around it, to even use it to benefit her. Her sadness made her act wildly. And it was overwhelming at times. There were nights when my mother cried so hard I thought she was mentally ill. It was from this same sadness though that she manifested her sense of compassion, which is why, as a minister, she was so adored by her congregation.

My aunt's sadness, on the other hand, was a very clingy sadness. It needed to be coddled. She was constantly pouting. It infected her whole being. It baited you, then dug into you like a fish hook or tapeworm. Instead of creating compassion, it fed on it. It sucked it dry and chewed on it like a dog would a bone.

Toward the end of my mother's life, she had gone through great pains to distance herself from Aunty. It got to the point where we only saw her the day after Christmas. Even then, things were tense between her and my mother.

"I'm sorry," she kept saying. "I didn't mean to ruin your night like this."

"You're not," I would assure her.

And then she would look at my mother.

"Well... Chris, I know you don't want me doing my laundry here anymore, but since it's the holiday, figured that maybe I could do a load or two..."

"No," my mother said. "No, Hilda, you can't."

At the time I couldn't understand why my mother was being so cold to her. It was just laundry. Now I understood how much anxiety Aunty's games could cause. I know now how courageous it was of my mother to not take the bait.

Aunty was gone for a little under an hour. When she came back I was in the kitchen waiting for her. Harold was wet. Most likely she had taken him to the ocean.

"Aunty, what the hell was that?"

"What was what honey?"

"Aunty, you were just out apartment hunting in the middle of the fucking night. That's crazy. Tell me what the hell's going on."

She started pacing. I got up and approached her. As soon as she saw that I was near her she grabbed onto me and started sobbing. I held and kissed her forehead. I tried to speak gently to her.

"Aunty, what the hell's going on?"

"I just want to be good to you! I just want to make this place nice for you! But, I keep messing things up!"

"No you don't. It's not like that Aunty! It's not like that at all! Think about all the milkshakes you get me."

I heard and felt her laugh against my chest.

"Oh Dustin," she said. "You're such a silly goose."

16

I hoped things would get better after that night; I would be able to take care of her, but it was more exhausting than I would have imagined. This woman drained me. Everything she said made me feel anxious. It was always the dog and her job and the dog and her job and did I want some ice cream...

I have never been so cold to someone as I was to this woman. No matter how devastated she acted, no matter how hard she cried, I would just sit there, going about my business, like she was a dog, begging for food.

One night she came home with a cake. It was an ice cream cake from Carvel. It was shaped like a whale.

"What's that for?" I asked.

"Well, it's my birthday so I figured I might as well buy myself a cake," she said.

She offered me a slice.

"Ice cream cake is my favorite," I told her.

"I know," she said. "That's why I got it."

She cried as I ate the cake.

I could hear Harold outside hopping around and barking at things.

17

I had woken up at four and started watching
television. There was a *Star Trek* marathon on the SyFy
Network. At first I felt embarrassed that I was having such
a good time watching it. It wasn't even the original series,
or *The Next Generation*, it was some weird spin off staring
the guy from *Quantum Leap*. It was horrible. I had seen
better science fiction watching midgets fight on a talk show. I
decided that it was fine, that I was just doing more research.
Fuck it. Maybe there was something valuable to learn about
the way cheap sci-fi affects the brain of lonely men like me.
Maybe I could start learn to write for shit like this and make
some money.

When I was thirteen I was obsessed with *Star Trek*.
My room was covered in all this Trekkie paraphernalia. I
even had the blue prints for the original Enterprise.

My cousin Wayne lived in our grandmother's
basement. He tried to tell me that *Star Trek* wasn't actually
"cool" at all, that it was in fact very nerdy. I didn't believe
him. Then I went to my first convention. It was nothing
extravagant, just a small lecture given at Suffolk Community
College by a man who directed a couple of the early episodes.
There were only a few people in the audience; they were all
nerds, but these guys were nerdy in a way that was morbid

and almost on a freak show level. Three seats in the front row were taken up by one man. I had never seen someone that obese before. My parents were fat and so was my aunt and grandmother, but they were all functioning human beings. They weren't sexy, but they could walk down the street without people looking at them like freaks. This guy's fatness had forgotten about him a long time ago. His body looked like two eyes connected to a ball of flesh. Two geeks got mad at the speaker for talking badly about one of their favorite episodes. He had said that it was a rip-off of a *Twilight Zone* story. They freaked out and started trying to boo him off the stage. They were escorted out of the auditorium and I was left alone with the obese guy and his three chairs.

When I got home that night I called and apologized to my cousin and then swore off watching the show for good. I was determined not to become one of them.

Quitting was more difficult than I had imagined it would be. I found myself getting even more obsessed. My weekends were spent in my basement where I had built a mock bridge of the Star Ship. I would be down there for hours at a time, pretending to be Captain Kirk with most of my adventures ending by having sex with a Romulan. I had a weird thing for Romulans. It was something about their skin. They had this slightly golden tan to them. I liked to imagine they smelled like peanut butter.

It was a sad, sad, part of my life. Quitting *Star Trek* was a long, arduous battle. And now here I was, ten years later, watching the damn thing again, tempting a dark and desolate fate. That obese son of bitch from the convention was sitting in the front row of my heart, taking up three seats. The more I watched, the fatter he got. I had thought I was free of that kind of loneliness. I had watched four episodes already and I was ready for more. For dinner I had eaten an entire jar of peanut butter with a spoon. This was it. That man in my heart, who breathed so heavily, that was me, that was the future me and I was a fool to ever think I could be anything different. Zoe, all those strippers, that was only role playing. It was me pretending I could be a normal man. The adventure I had in the basement was the life I was destined to live. I would make Aunty my first officer. We would travel beyond the limits of the galaxy together.

The phone rang and I picked it up. It was Slim.
"Grimboli, what are you doing?"
"Research."
"Really?"
"Yes..."
I felt drugged. It was like I was trying to talk underwater.
"Grimboli. You ever been to the Friskies?"
"No."
"It's a club in Hampton Bays. We're going."
"But my research..."
"Grimboli, this is important. There is tons of women that love having sex when they're drunk."
"I haven't had sex in months."
"That's bad Grimboli."
"I don't even feel like a man anymore."
"Grimboli, get over to Milz's place at ten. We goin to pre- game then get to the club by eleven."
"But, I'm broke."
"Don't worry Grimboli Stromboli. I'll get you in for free. I knows people."
"Thanks Slim."
"No problem."
He had no idea that he had just saved me from a lonely and terrible fate. Most likely he was just using me for a ride, but I didn't care. I felt nothing but gratitude towards him.

18

"Jesus, look at Grimboli!" Milz yelled as I entered his room. "He's dressed like he just got back from 'Nam."

"Grimboli," Slim added. "Who dresses like that to a club?"

"I thought it looked hip hop."

"Yeah, maybe in Nineties."

"Or in 'Nam!"

They laughed. Slim passed me a handle of rum. I took a nice, long swig. It tasted good. By the time we left I had drank most of the bottle.

As I drove to the club Slim and Milz sat in the back seat dancing to Billy Joel. The car was filthy. Slim kept finding trash and throwing it at me to try and get me riled up. Milz was just mad about the mess.

"Grimboli, this is fucking nasty!" he kept yelling.

We got to the club around midnight. It took us an hour to get in. Slim had to call a friend that worked there. The guy didn't pick up. Slim called obsessively for a half hour. He finally answered. He said he would help us get in, but that we still had to wait in line. That took another hour. When we finally got to the door Slim whispered something in the bouncer's ear and then the gorilla angrily rushed us into the club.

The place was packed. Moving around was difficult. Ordering a drink was even worse. They had two bimbos pouring mixed drinks for the whole club. It was madness. All the drinks I ordered were watered down. Instead of a buzz, I got a stomach ache. It felt like my stomach was mad at me for tricking it and making it think it was consuming alcohol. I had borrowed twenty dollars from my aunt and I felt bad for wasting it on such weak ass drinks, so I spent the rest of the night scumming, which is the art of going around and taking the last sip of discarded beverages. This did not help my stomach ache.

Eventually, I gave up on drinking and decided to dance. The dancing helped my stomach. It loosened me up, got me sweating. Most of the men in the crowd didn't dance. They just stood there as the women grinded against them. I was alone and trying to move smoothly, but I was acting more like some crazed witchdoctor trying to call forth the rain gods.

Slim grabbed me out of the crowd.

"Grimboli, you look straight crazy out there. You look like a fat Michael Jackson."

"I know. I'm really good at dancing."

"Listen, I need to introduce you to Big Teddy."

Big Teddy was the largest man in the club. He was the size of the guy from the Star Trek convention, only he was dressed better. Much better and he smelled good too.

Slim introduced us. He shook my hand. Both our hands were very soft and massive. My hand looked like a dime in a baseball glove.

"What's with all that shit on your face?"

He was referring to my beard.

"No girl gonna wanta kiss on a face covered in all that shit, man."

"What if they're drunk?" I asked.

He didn't hear me.

"I said 'what if they are drunk?'"

Big Ted shook his head and stumbled off.

I spent the rest of the night sitting at the bar. At about three the club started to clear out. The bartender caught me scumming drinks. She felt bad for me so she gave me a beer on the house.

A girl came down and sat next to me. I didn't recognize her at first. She blended in too much with the rest of the girls. But then I saw those eyes and they were filled with wet and molested fireworks. It was Mel-Mel, that crazy bitch.

"Hey, Mel-Mel, how are you doing?" I yelled over to her.

She didn't recognize me.

"Who the fuck are you?" she yelled.

"I'm Grimboli. I gave you and some other lady a ride to a bar a while back."

I remembered the rest of the night, the fighting and the yelling and the shot gun and I decided not to dig any deeper into the girl's memory. She didn't remember me or the rest of that night and that was probably for the best.

"You should buy me a drink," she said.

"I'm broke," I said.

"Oh, poor baby!"

"You look good," I told her.

"You're a fucking, little bitch!" she replied.

I started to walk away, but she grabbed me and pulled me to her and started kissing me. She didn't bite me this time; she filled my mouth with tongue and she moaned and her hands felt my belly and my cock.

Big Teddy came up behind her. He looked angry.

"Come on Mel-Mel; let's get going."

He took her by the arm, then led her off.

Slim and Milz were at the other end of the bar. They had seen the whole thing and were laughing hysterically.

60

I didn't care. It had been a long time since someone had touched my penis. I felt good.

We went back to the club that next Friday. This time I attempted to look nice. I wore a sweatshirt my father had given me for Christmas. The tag was still on and it smelled like a LL BEAN store. I felt like a stud, like all I had to do was look at a girl and her pussy would bubble over with passion.

"Holy fuck, look at Grimboli!" Slim yelled when he saw me.

"Look at that sweatshirt!" Milz added. "He looks like fucking Bill Cosby."

They laughed.

I started dancing. I still had a little confidence and I was desperate to take advantage of it.

There was a younger looking girl on the dance floor who seemed unoccupied. She was sexy. She was wearing a denim jumpsuit that clung to her body as tightly as her own flesh. The front of the outfit was unbuttoned just enough so I could see a birth mark she had on her right breast. She was short and had a tight ass.

I made eye contact with her and smiled. She smiled. It wasn't a very flirtatious smile, but it was enough. I rushed up behind her and started grinding my crotch against her sweet rump.

"Stop." she said. "I'm trying to dance with my friends."

Who dresses like that to just dance with her friends, I thought. And then I saw a guy come up to her. He was like every other wop in the place. He wore pre-faded jeans and his hair was so gelled up that he looked like Sonic the Hedge Hog. The girl started dancing and the giant Dago just stood there like she was shinning his shoes. This was a man to these girls. This is what got them horny.

My self-esteem had gotten a thorough ass kicking by the whole ordeal. I stood there watching them, feeling so low that it took considerable effort to not just lie down on the floor in a fetal position and go to sleep.

Luckily the DJ turned on some Biggie. I loved Biggie. That nigger could make the ugliest, sloppiest loser feel as infamous as goddamn Scarface. Women weren't repulsed by me; they were afraid of me. My dick was a machine gun covered in cocaine.

I continued dancing. I stared at all the girl with eyes that chewed them up like a dog chews a sock. One girl started dancing with me. She was big and black and she didn't dance well, but she rubbed her big ass against me and it felt warm and raunchy and good. Again, Big Teddy came up and, like with Mel-Mel, he grabbed her by the arm and dragged her out of the club. I walked up to Milz and Slim who had been watching me.

"What does that fucker have against me? What the fuck did I ever do to him?"

"Nothing man, that girl had just snuck in," Milz told me.

"Yeah big Grim, that girl that you were dancing with is a retard. She just lives down the street and every once in a while she tries to sneak in here."

"Are you sure?"

"Yes, I'm sure. Grimboli, you were practically hooking up with someone who is mentally handicap."

"Shit, the lighting is so bad, I couldn't see her. I..."

"Grimboli, I thought you said you love retards... "

"What?"

"I thought you said that you hang out with that one kid... what's his name?"

"Samuel."

"That's right, Samuel."

"I used to baby sit him. He's ten years old."

"Didn't you say that he shits his pants and you have to clean him?"

"Sure, I have to wipe his butt and stuff."

"Well, really, if you think about it there is no difference."

"Difference between what?"

"Wiping that kids ass and what you just did to that girl on the dance floor."

Slim nearly toppled over laughing.

I told him I wanted to leave. He said that he and Milz were going to stay, that he had found another ride.

As I drove home I thought about Samuel. I hadn't seen him in a while. Baby sitting that crazy little fucker always made me feel decent about things. He had a big belly that looked almost pregnant and he had a laugh that just rolled and rolled and rolled.

His mother went to my father's church. I had been avoiding church. It wasn't the building or God that scared me off, but my father and his sermons. They were so sweet, so direct and sentimental. They always made me cry. I didn't want this. I didn't want to cry.

19

That night I dreamt about my mother. I was at the creek where I had put her ashes. I was swimming with a statue of her in my arms. It was big and heavy, but while I was in the water it was practically weightless. Still, I ended up dropping it. The thing just slipped out of my arms. I dipped my face in the water and I watched it float down. The creek had no bottom. It was just going to keep falling like that, like a sky diver that never needs to open up their shoot.

I pulled my head out of the water. There was a woman bathing on the other end of the swimming hole. She was naked and large and very soft looking. I swam over to her. It was my mother.

"Let's bathe together," she said.

Instead of bathing, we ended up having sex. My dick was tiny like a baby, so it couldn't reach. I ended up just humping her ass cheeks.

When I woke up it was ten in the morning and I felt like a dry turd hanging off of one of God's ass hairs. It was the first time I had woken up at a decent hour in months. I decided to go back to bed though, hoping this time I wouldn't dream about fucking my mother.

20

Ironically Sally, Samuels's mother, called me. In the background I could hear Samuel crying. His tears leaked out of the phone, into my ears and scraped my bones. It sounded horrible. Loneliness and frustration festered in this kid like a pile of trapped rats.

"He misses you," she said to me.

"I would love to see him."

"Well, how 'bout you come and pick him up this Saturday. I have to go see my mother up in Queens and I could really use a cheap baby sitter."

I agreed.

On Saturday I picked Samuel up and took him for a drive. He was easier to deal with when he was in a car. As I drove him around we would make noises at each other. Initially we would just make animal sounds. He would growl at me and then I would caw like a bird. Over time the noises got stranger. There would be a lot a beeping and gurgling like a machine that was drowning in slime. Time flew by. We would go back and forth like this for hours.

That day I took him out for pizza. We ran into the Rugrats. I thought they would be excited to see Samuel. I thought they would find him to be hysterical. But, like most men, retarded people made them nervous. Rarely had I seen them act so shy. Usually they would stand around and joke with me, but that day they barely said hello and then they ran off.

"Oh-my-golly..." Samuel said in a frog-like growl.

"You're telling me," I said. "Let's go get some pizza."

Samuel ate his pizza upside down. It made the process very messy. His mother, one of the few people that could decipher his mumbling, swore that he ate it this way so the cheese, the good part, touched his tongue first.

When we were done his chin was glossy with pizza oil.

"You look shiny." I told him.

He giggled.

"Etch-ah!" he mumbled at me.

"What the fuck is a etcher?" I said.

He growled. I shouldn't of teased him. Not being able to talk was obviously incredibly frustrating.

"Atchup!" he yelled.

"I'm sorry, I don't understand you," I told him.

"Etchup..."

"Did you say ketchup?"

He nodded.

"Oh you want ketchup. I get it now."

Ketchup was what he called hamburgers. Again, his mother said this was because he thought ketchup was the best part and like with the cheese on the pizza, he liked to focus most of his attention on it.

"Sorry Samuel, but you can't have any ketchup you just had pizza."

As I was driving him home I noticed him rubbing his butt into the seat. I knew what this meant. He had to shit. Grinding his ass was his way of trying to push the shit back.

We couldn't make it to a bathroom on time, so I ended up having to pull over and change his diaper. It was a gross. Ten year olds take really stinky shits. It was not like changing a baby's diaper. Samuel had shits that were so slimy and foul that it practically seemed to be bubbling. While wiping his ass I made sure to plug my nose with toilet paper. I had an entire roll up each nostril. It hung from my nose and made me look like I had a big white beard. Samuel thought this was hilarious. He laughed and laughed. It was either that or the fact that I was wiping his ass that made him laugh so hard, I really couldn't tell.

When we got back in the car he started making noises again. I was tired. I didn't want to play anymore. But if I didn't, he would have a tantrum. So, I started beeping and growling at him again. I made noises that only the strangest creature could ever create. And he laughed then made his own sounds that were equally as bizarre. By the time I had dropped him off I found it hard to communicate normally.

"How was Samuel?" Sally asked. "I hope he wasn't too much of a handful."

I told her he was fine, but my voice kept jumping into the tone I used when making my machine noises.

"Are you all right?" she asked.

"I'm fine," I told her. "Beep."

21

My driver's license had expired. I needed to get to the DMV, but I kept sleeping in too late. At this point I had gotten into the habit of sleeping till five. Things were dark. I had run out of money and was too lazy to get a job, so I wasn't leaving the house much. It was just me and Aunty. I felt like I belonged to her now. Like I was a strange creature that only woke up at night and growled at her until she fed it. Even Harold's life seemed more fulfilling than the one I was leading. At least he saw day light. He spent most of his day barking at walls or as Aunty believed, talking to my mother's spirit, but whatever, he seemed to be having a good time.

One day I came up with a plan. I decided to take a handful of Tylenol PM at about eight. This would put me to sleep by nine. That way I would wake up at a normal time. My hope was that this would set me on the path to a normal sleeping schedule, but even if it failed in the long term, I would at least get to the DMV.

I didn't dream that night. All I remembered was taking the pills, lying in bed and waiting. Next thing I knew I was awake and it was six in the morning and I could hear the birds chirping. Those birds, that normally sounded like they were mocking my insomnia, sounded so much more pleasant now, like they were flirting with me and tempting me to get on with the day.

I was excited and jumped in my car and headed for the DMV.

22

I couldn't believe it; the DMV was closed. Fuck. I had driven all this way and it was closed. I had woken up too early. Now what? I decided to just drive around. Eventually I made my way down the North Fork and then took the ferry over to Shelter Island where my father's church was. I had trouble finding his apartment, but when I drove by his church I noticed that the parking lot was packed. There was some sort of function being held. I was curious about what was drawing such a crowd and I also hoped to find my father.

I walked in and heard singing coming from the sanctuary. An older woman came out of the bathroom. She looked frail. Her hair was short and curly and she smelled like powder.

"What's going on here today?" I asked.

"Church," she said.

"I know this is a church, but what's going on?"

"Church. It's Sunday morning. The service is just ending."

I couldn't believe it. It was already Sunday? No wonder the DMV was closed. Was I this out of touch?

The service ended. My father found me waiting in his office. He was a large man. Standing and preaching made him sweat. By the time he got to his office he was drenched. I told him about how I had stumbled upon the church not knowing it was Sunday and he laughed.

It was good to see him. It was good to be in his office again. He kept things so clean and organized. There were pictures of me everywhere. Most of them were from when I was a child. One was of Zoe and me.

"Why do you still have that picture up?" I asked, pointing to it. "You feel the need to remind your congregation that your weirdo son still likes women?"

"No! Why would you think that? I just think it's a nice picture is all. I can take it down if it upsets you."

"Don't worry about it."

I enjoyed seeing him. Still, I found myself trying to start a fight. Our fights were epic. They covered a wide array of subjects, like god and sex and my dead mother. This fight started with me whining about how lonely I was. My father suggested that I take advantage of this time I had to myself and use it for self reflection. This made me irate.

"You didn't take much time off when mom died!"

"Dustin what are you talking about?"

"You got married to Loo, what, like a year later? And now you're telling me that I got to be single!"

"Dustin, I'm not telling you anything."

"We don't even have a grave dad!"

"What?"

"A grave. We don't even have a fucking grave. I can't even go and visit her grave like a normal person and bring her flowers."

"Dustin, why do we always have to fight?"

"Because it's what we do dad,; we fight."

"Life is hard enough as it is without us having to fight all the time. Is it asking too much for us to just have a nice visit?"

"It's good we fight about this shit! What's obnoxious is

your need to constantly fight about why we fight all the time. Just accept it. Fuck. Mom never got like this. That woman could go on forever with a good fight."

"Dustin. I'm not your mother."

"I'm not saying…"

"Dustin," he said. "I'm sorry, your mother would love to get into heated debates with you. And I know, she could go on for hours. I just don't have that kind of energy."

And that was how the fights always ended. All it took was the word "I'm sorry" and I would buckle over in tears. My father thought it was because he had brought up my dead mom, but that wasn't it at all. It was that he said he was sorry, that is what did it to me. There was a deeply hurt and deeply spoiled side of me that was desperate for an apology and I didn't know what for, but as soon as I heard those words come out of my dad's mouth… I was broken.

A member of his congregation came in and found me on the floor in a fetal position, sobbing.

"He'll be fine," I heard my father say.

The woman left and then I began to sob even harder.

"The day started out so nicely!" I wailed. "I woke up early and everything!"

23

A while back we put my mom's ashes in the Schoharie Creek in upstate New York. It was where her father had drowned and it was also where she had taught me how to swim. We went there frequently when I was young. I had never seen her more content than when she was sun bathing on one of the big muddy rocks that lay at the edge of her favorite swimming hole.

It had been a long time since we had visited that place. So, my father, after I got off the ground and stopped crying, suggested that we travel up there, stay with Aunt Gretchen and pay our respects to my mother.

I didn't share with him the dream I had about her recently.

I told Aunty about the trip. At first she acted very supportive.

"I think it will be nice for you and your dad to get away!" she said.

Then her mood soured.

"Geez, I haven't talked to your dad in a while. The only time I ever hear from him is when he asks for the rent money. And now he says he isn't going to pay for the bottled water to get brought here. And I can't afford it. So I guess I'll just have to do without water."

"What about water from the sink," I suggested.

"No, I don't like the way it tastes…"

"I'm sure you'll be fine," I said to her.

She had sat down on the floor and was playing with Harold.

"People need water to survive," she said.

"Aunty, I'm sure you'll be fine."

"Yeah…well…"

My father and I left that weekend, leaving early in the morning and arriving at my aunts mid day. First thing, we headed down to the creek. It was as I had remembered it. The water was green, murky and soft; the cliff hung over it with sleepy affection. It was nice to be there, but it didn't provoke the emotion I expected it to. I had wanted to break down and weep, but I felt none of that sweet craziness stirring in me.

My father suggested that we get a plaque that could be embedded into one of the rocks.

"It can have your mom's face on it," he said.

"No," I said. "I don't think it would be worth it."

Aunt Gretchen made us pasta for dinner. She used tomatoes and basil from her garden. It was simple but delicious. When you have good ingredients you don't have to use a complex recipe. The meal was perfect.

My father and I did most of the talking. Gretchen wasn't the most sociable woman.

She and my father went to bed at nine and even though my sleeping schedule had improved, I still had trouble falling asleep before the clock reached the double digits.

I lied in bed feeling restless. At about midnight I

decided to go for a walk to waste some energy.

I walked down to the bridge that overlooked a more shallow part of the creek. When I was young I used to go there and pace back and forth and I would imagine robots fighting in a desolate wasteland. The robots would be as rusty as the bridge, but they would be fierce. I liked imagining them grappling with each other as they fell from the sky and into the creek. Though I had been told that the creek is only fifteen feet deep, I would imagine its depths as being endless. Awkward creatures would gather around and watch them as they fought on the murky bottom.

That night, I tried conjuring up some of those old fantasies and they came at first, but then faded. I had trouble focusing on the image of the robots. As soon as they started wrestling my mind would jump to images of sex. Sex was all I fantasized about now. No more robots. It was like being a sports fanatic who had traded all his baseball cards for just one Babe Ruth, signed. Sure, nothing better than the Great Bambino, but was it worth giving up the entire collection?

I stared at the creek. Just like when I was young, it seemed as deep as the ocean. If anyone would have asked me right then how deep it was I would have had to lie and said it was at least a couple hundred feet deep, maybe deeper.

On my walk back I saw a woman outside her home. She was short and old.

"Excuse me!" she yelled over to me. "Can you come over here for a moment! I need your help!"

I ran over to her as quick as I could, thinking she was hurt. But as soon as I got close I could tell that she was fine, she just seemed a bit out of breath. Next to her was a giant log that had been tipped on its side.

"Are you strong?" she asked.

"I guess so," I told her.

"Well, I need you to move this log."

I bent down and started trying to push the log. It was heavy and the shed she wanted me to push it to was up a hill.

"It's... it's... too heavy!" I told her.

The old woman bent down and started pushing with me. As we pushed we started growling, as if to conjure up some old forgotten strength. We made it part way up the hill then gave up.

"I'm sorry," I said.

"Yeah, well, I guess I'll just try again tomorrow," she said.

And then, without out a goodbye, she waddled off and into her home.

In the morning Aunt Gretchen made us breakfast sandwiches. Usually I am a firm believer that egg sandwiches need to be lathered in American cheese. But these sandwiches didn't even have cheese on them and they tasted wonderful.

After eating we went back to the creek. The water was high. In the summer the creek could be very tranquil. The water falls poured down gently so you could bathe under them. Now they were raging and exploding into foam. There were rapids on the other end of the swimming hole. If we jumped in and braved the cold, these rapids would suck us up like action figures flushed down a toilet.

"Are you ready to start heading home?" my father asked.

I nodded.

Home was six hours away, but with my father driving, it took eleven. He only used the back roads and would frequently pull over to take pictures. We rarely got out of the car. I had never met someone who loved looking at nature so much, but hated walking through it. Even when he took pictures he just reached his hand out the window.

We had a few good fights. None that ended with me crying, but still they were epic none the less. We fought about movies mainly. I didn't like the movies he liked to watch. Sentimental movies were fine, but he liked stuff that was so sweet it made your teeth hurt to watch them.

"Why are you so critical of me?" he asked.

"I can't help it."

"I wish you could just enjoy me a little bit."

"I do," I told him. "I enjoy you more than anyone else I know."

"Well, it sure doesn't seem like it."

"That's fine," I said.

I had him pull over so I could take a piss. We didn't fight much after that. It's hard to fight after taking a piss. Pissing made everything feel serene.

It was strange to see how wet and lively everything looked. Winter had been so mild that I had forgotten to notice when spring came. My father hadn't though. He loved flowers the way women love flowers. He saw emotion in them. What I liked best was the wet wood and the sound of water moaning under a bridge, things that didn't need emotion because their endurance and consistency held something more important, like the sound of someone sleeping near you, not necessarily a girlfriend, but anyone, even just some drunk friend on your couch.

24

I got home late. I was tired. Too tired to bother trying to sneak through the house quietly. First I woke Harold; he barked at me like I was a criminal. Then Aunty woke up. She wanted to know why I was home so late. Her voice was stern. I didn't like this. When she was done she apologized.

"I was just concerned is all. I didn't mean to sound like I was trying to be you mother."

She didn't sound like my mother. She sounded like a jealous girlfriend.

25

I got a call from my friend Gorcoff. He was going to art school up in Maine. He had just finished finals and wanted to come down to visit for a few weeks. I told him he was welcome. I thought of Gorcoff as being like a brother. His own family was neglectful, so when he wanted to visit home he visited me.

Aunty did not feel affectionate toward Gorcoff, like I did.

"He wears those boots," she said. "And he just clunks around the house like nobody's business. Sometimes I'll wake up to him just a clunking away. And he never does the dishes. And he curses like a sailor."

I would plead with her to be more gracious with Gorcoff.

"He has no family," I told her. "The son of a bitch needs us. Kid had it rough. If my mom was around she would have loved Gorcoff."

I figured that would get her. People used that tactic on me all the time. Whenever someone wanted me to feel bad about something I was doing they would say, "Now what would your mom say?"

This didn't work on me and it didn't seem to work on

Aunty either. She seemed determined to dislike Gorcoff. She respected the idea of my father paying for his college and she even liked the idea of making him family, but only as an idea. Beyond that, she was completely sour toward his presence in our world.

Gorcoff showed up late on a Saturday night. It was good to see him. He loved me with such sheer force and although, he was much smaller, he was strong and able to pick me up easily. His curly Jew-fro rubbed into my face.

"Aw Grimboli, you whore, I fuck'n missed you! How the fuck are you, goddamn it?"

"You're hurting me!" I yelled jokingly.

"Aw, you can take it! You're a savage; you're a beast! Look at you!"

He hugged me again.

"How's school?" I asked.

"Aw, she best! Nothing but tons of slice to be had."

Slice was slang for girl. Gorcoff was infamous for his use of slang and for talking about himself in the third person.

"Ol' Gorcoff, he loves to hit all sorts of leg. Loves. But really, ol' Gorcoff, he just likes to be loved. Basically, Gorcoff just wants something nice. A nice girl. That's all."

Gorcoff was filled with contradictions. That was part of the poetry of his speech. He constantly monologued on about whatever he was thinking and it was hard for him to keep track of what he was saying or who he was at times.

"Gorcoff's an artist. Not meant for the world of women. Women hate. They hate. All I want, seriously, all I want sometimes is to just wake up, eat my oatmeal, paint a little, do what I love, and then the woman, always has to get threatened and start harping on me, trying to plan my whole fucking day. I can barely handle it."

"Gorcoff, I haven't been with a woman in a long, long time."

He seemed concerned.

"Why the fuck haven't you been hitting any? You're a good looking guy? You're funny."

"I know," I said. "But I've been hanging out with the Rugrats and all the girls they hang out with are just too young."

"Do you like any of these girl?"

"Sure."

"Ok, see what you need to do, what ol' Gorcoff would do is, just go for it. Fuck it right? What do you have to lose?"

I didn't know how to tell him that they simply seemed repulsed by me; they rarely even spoke to me and that there really wasn't anything to pursue. And that I didn't want to go to prison over some chick who wasn't even old enough to fucking drive yet.

To switch topics I brought up Zoe. She always got him excited.

"God damn Zoe was one insanely high quality piece. But she was bad to you bro. She's a no good rotten piece of filth."

"Naw, she wasn't that bad."

"I know, I know, she was best. God, I'd slam it if I could. She was a complete smoke show. She was a god damned squirt wagon. I'd god damn kill myself if I lost something like that..."

His eyes focused on something that was on the kitchen table.

"What the fuck is this?"

"What's what?" I asked.

He showed me a little piece of paper. On it was a note written by my aunt. "I don't know how I can afford groceries it said." There were more notes. They were all over the kitchen. "I feel insecure." One said. Another complained about missing an episode of her favorite soap opera. The craziest was about Maude. "Why did she have to die," it said.

"I wish I could offer my life in return for hers."

"Who wrote this?" Gorcoff asked.

"Aunty."

"Fuck off! Aunty wrote this!"

"Be quiet," I told him. "She's sleeping in the living room."

"No way!"

"Yes! That's where she sleeps every night!"

"And here we are talking like a couple of ex-cons and she can hear?"

I nodded.

He looked back over the notes.

"This is the wildest shit I have ever heard of."

The more Gorcoff heard about how I had been living the more concerned he got.

He seemed determined to pull me out of my funk. His first objective was to get me in shape.

"Nothing makes you feel better," he said. "The happiness level after working out is best."

It got him excited.

"Grimboli, it's going to be best. We're going to get you jacked to the max. You're going to be huge. Look at these arms, look at these gun boats. Aw. We're going to make you massive."

I borrowed some money from my father and then bought a cheap weight bench from K-mart. We worked out daily. It was addictive. I didn't want to do anything else.

At first it was awkward. I felt pathetic. My muscles were as strong as a teenage, anorexic girl.

But, I improved quickly.

When we weren't exercising, we were eating. Gorcoff was always hungry.

"We need fuel," he would say. "Aw it's best. Fuel. Meats best. Meat delivers."

We spent the rest of our time driving around looking at the rich women who had come to the Hamptons for the summer. He called attractive women Charley. At his school he had a buddy named Charley who was always staring at women really blatantly. So whenever you stared a woman he called it Charleying. And he also called women Charley. "Look at all that Charley," he would say. Or "Yeah I saw you Charleying that sweet piece of Charley." I liked this. It reminded me of soldiers in the Vietnam War. We were constantly looking for Charley the same way they were except we didn't want to shot or kill them. We just wanted to fuck them.

Things with Aunty were tense. She was especially grumpy whenever she was around Gorcoff.

"Maybe I should leave?" Gorcoff asked.

This made me furious. Gorcoff had rejuvenated me. Because of him I could now bench the weight of a small woman and I ate steak and felt like I deserved it. It was...best.

Gorcoff was an artist. Most of the time he liked to paint zombies. He didn't paint them eating people though. Usually, the zombies were just roaming some sort of barren landscape, looking like a dog in a desert.

One time Gorcoff left his brushes in the sink. Aunty was convinced that they were going to stain the sink permanently. She kept looking and shaking her head.

"It's going to be fine," I told her. "I'm sure the paint will come out eventually. And even if it doesn't, it's really no big deal."

"It's just I know how important this sink was to your mother," she said.

I grabbed her by the arms. "My mother is dead, and dead people don't care about sinks,"

She ran out of the room sobbing.

"I don't know how much more of this I can take,"

Gorcoff said.

I agreed. But in a way Aunty was right. The sink was my mother's. This whole house was hers. We lived in a tomb. And the dead don't come back to life like they do in the movies. No, they sleep on the couch and moan so deeply that it gets in your skin, making you feel like you're dead too.

A few days later Gorcoff decided to leave. There was a girl he knew who lived upstate. They had been talking a lot and he wanted to visit. On the day he planned on leaving he woke me up at six in the morning so he could catch the earliest train possible. Waking up that early was not easy for me; I was still drunk from the night before. My head and my lungs and my guts felt like sewage. If I was to take a breathalyzer, I would a clog the thing with cigarette butts and a beer cans.

"Come on!" he begged. "I gotta go!"

I was so tired that I didn't bother getting dressed. I got in the mini-van wearing nothing but a t-shirt and my dirty underwear.

Gorcoff thought this was hilarious.

"This is the wildest thing I have ever seen," he said. I liked making Gorcoff laugh. It was rewarding. He laughed the way Samuel laughed. He laughed with his belly and his heart and his balls.

We started down the road.

"What's that sound?" Gorcoff asked.

"I don't know."

"Holy shit! Something is in the engine!" he yelled.

"Something what...?"

As I looked over to see what the hell he was talking about and accidentally turned the steering wheel too far and ran us off the road and into a tree. Gorcoff went flying into the dash board as my head bounced from the steering wheel to the head rest and back to the steering wheel like a basket ball. Blood dripped down my head and into my eye. I was cut but it didn't hurt.

"Are you ok?" Gorcoff asked.

"I'm fine."

We stumbled out of the car. The tree had cracked and was lying on top of the van. Suddenly a cat flew out from under the van and wobbled away into the fog.

A woman walked by with her dog.

"Are you two alright?" she asked.

Gorcoff looked over at me. I was in my underwear and bleeding and we just missed killing a cat. We started laughing so wildly that we fell on the ground. The woman walked away, nervously.

"Grimboli!" Gorcoff yelled. "Look, we only made it a block away from the house!"

"It's evil," I told him. "That house is evil. It doesn't want us to leave."

"We're doomed."

"Do you still want to try and make your train?"

"Naw, fuck it. I'll go tomorrow."

"She best," I told him.

Over time I had picked up his slang. It was very contagious.

"What did you just say?" he asked.

"I said she best."

"She is best."

26

The Rugrats called and said they wanted to go to that club in Hampton Bays. Normally Gorcoff didn't like to go to out to clubs, but the accident had riled him up and he was ready to celebrate the fact that we had survived. It didn't take much to make us feel manly. The accident was small. The word accident made it sound severe. It was more of a goof. Regardless, Gorcoff and I felt as rugged as two men that had just sailed through a hurricane. We wanted to go out and drink and tell people about our adventures, about the old woman who refused to help us and tree we had cut in two and the cat who nearly got chopped up. Sure, we were only a block away from our house, but that only went to further prove how treacherous our lives truly were.

A night out with the Rugrats seemed perfect. The only problem was that I had knocked out the van's left headlight in the accident. I didn't want to get pulled over because the vehicle wasn't registered and I, most likely, would be very drunk while driving it.

The Rugrats were appalled when they saw what I had done to solve this problem.

"What the fuck is this?" Jesse asked. "Grimboli, did you just tape a bunch of flashlights to the side of your mom's van?"

"I think it might work," I told them. "We drove by a cop on our way here and he didn't pull us over. I think we might have fooled him."

"I hate this," Milz said.

"Grimboli, this is fully horrible. We have a girl with us."

"Girls like messy guys," I assured them.

But I could tell by the way they were looking at me that that wasn't true.

"I hate this!" Milz repeated.

He got even more upset when he got in and stepped on a stray can of carpet cleaner. It sprayed foam on his shoes and pants.

"Grimboli, if this shit stains, I am going to beat the shit out of you."

"That's fine," I said.

I acted aloof in hopes that it might alleviate some of the tension, but it didn't work. Instead, I just made people more agitated. It was Gorcoff that smoothed things over. The Rugrats thought he was funny. He told them about the accident and the cat and had them all in hysterics. His version of the story was more comedic than mine. He described us as being like Chris Farley and David Spade. It was obvious who was Chris Farley

My version was much more dramatic.

"I thought he was dead," I told them. "For one moment I considered the possibility that I had killed Gorcoff. Oh god, I don't know how I could have lived with myself."

"Why does Grimboli always got to be so serious?" they complained.

We got to the club early. There wasn't much of a line. It didn't take long to get to the door, but the cover charge had gone up and Big Teddy refused to vouch for us. Jesse and Slim spent an hour on their cell phones trying to call people who could weasel us in.

"We got girls with us!" they would yell. "We got girls who love to hook up! You know I'm good! You know I got your back! Shit baby, I always got your back! Now what? Now you say you can't hook me up? Shit..."

As they made these calls, more and more people showed up at the club. The line became massive.

Finally, they gave up and we headed home.

One of the girls was named Carmen. She was tall and goofy looking and she wore her shirt so loose her nipples would pop out and her dress was so high up that you could hear her pussy puckering its lips and blowing kisses at you. She had long, curly hair and a big forehead. I sat in the back with her sharing a handle of whiskey. A kid they called Black Jesse sat on the other side. He would talk over me trying to flirt with her.

"Damn girl," he said. "Do you realize how good you look in that skirt! I mean, you look good!"

I would then chime in, mocking him, but twisting it just a tad.

"You do look very lovely!"

"Shit girl," Black Jesse went on, "you just make me feel nasty as a dog!"

"I too, find your beauty to be inspiring," I said.

She laughed. Carmen liked our little routine.

But as I drank more of the whiskey I got more and more belligerent.

"Kiss me!" I begged her.

"I can't," she said. "I got a boyfriend."

"What?!"

"I got a boyfriend."

"That's silly!"

She let me put my hand on her leg.

"I almost died today! I need a kiss damn't! Have some

88

fucking mercy!"

"I can't!"

"Just kiss my face! Kiss my ears! Kiss my belly!"

I lifted up my shirt and showed her my big white belly. Black Jesse started laughing.

"Holy shit you guys! Grimboli gettin' crazy back here!"

The van went quiet. Everyone was listening.

"Kiss my ear! I want your kiss to go directly to my brain! I want it to sit in there and make me horny in my dreams!"

Everyone laughed.

"Please, just kiss me."

"I can't."

"Why?"

"I got a boyfriend."

"Where is he right now?"

"His parents grounded him."

"Holy moly. How old are you?"

"Sixteen."

"That's great! I'm only fourteen!"

"No you're not! You look at least thirty!"

"Shit, I do? I'm so embarrassed."

"Well then, how old are you?" she asked.

"Twenty two. I'm in the middle school of adult hood."

"You dress like a dad."

"Yeah, I've heard that before."

"You know what, even though your kinda a geek and shit, I bet in the sack you're like Ron Jeremy."

"Who?"

"You know, Ron Jeremy, that fat, gopher looking guy who was in all those porn; the guy who makes all those bad jokes while he's fucking all those women."

"Ok. I know who you are talking about."

"I bet you're like that dude."

"You do?"

"Yeah I bet you got a big ol' dick."

"I don't really. I got huge balls though."

"Oh man that's nasty."

I looked out the window and noticed that we were on a dirt road heading deep into the woods.

"Hey, Gorcoff, where are we going?"

"Shanty town!"

Shanty town was a village made out of shacks, dilapidated vans and boats. It was hidden in the woods in Bridgehampton. Kalish used to take me there when we were younger. He would try to scare me by telling me that a family of inbred mutants lived there. We would drive there on his quad. The place was huge. There were dozens of elaborate shacks on either side of the dirt road. As we drove through I would see the shadows of people peeking out through boarded up windows. They were rarely outside of the shacks. Once I saw a little naked Mexican girl picking dandelions. I heard her mother yell out to her. She sounded terrified.

On our way back home I asked Kalish to tell the real story behind Shanty town. He told me that Mexican immigrants lived there until they found a job and were able to live somewhere else. Even though I knew the truth, I still liked going there, especially at night. In the moon light, the place looked like something out of a horror story, something HP Lovecraft or Stephen King would write. Even into my late teenager years I found this place terrifying. That was rare for a teenager. Adolescence turns boys into the worse kind of cynics. They lose the ability to suspend their disbelief, to get scared, or amazed by anything. But this place scared the shit out me and that felt like a sweet, sweet gift to feel that way again.

"I don't want to go to Shanty town!" I yelled. "I'm too drunk. Nothing scary when you're drunk!"

"We're going to get drunk with the Mexicans," Jesse said.

"Arreeeeeba!" Slim howled.

The car came to a screeching halt, whipping the dust
into the headlights. When it cleared all we saw was a fence
and a sign warning trespassers to keep out.

"Where's Shanty town?" Slim asked.

"It's gone," Gorcoff said.

We all got out of the car and peered through the fence
hoping to see remnants of the shacks that had stood just a
hundred feet beyond the fence. There was nothing but fog
creeping off the ground restlessly, still not familiar with so
much open space.

Gorcoff drove us away slowly.

"Grimboli, can we go drink some more at your place?"
Jesse asked.

"Sure," I said. "We just have to be quiet."

When we got to my house we filed out of the van
then sat in my drive way in a circle like we were playing
duck-duck-goose. It was late and every plan we made had
backfired. None of us were ready to end the night. There was
a strange perseverance in us. If we were alive in the early
1800's we would have been the ones going west and fighting
Indians and getting drunk and digging up gold. It was boys
like us, filled with that sweet idiot-hunger for glory that made
this country what it was today.

"Grimboli, let's go inside. It's kinda chilly out here,"
someone suggested.

"Yeah, I want to eat snacks," someone else said.

"We can't," I told them. "My aunt's in there."

"We'll be super quiet."

"No you don't get it; she sleeps on the couch. It would
be impossible not to wake her."

"Grimboli!" Jesse said. "I'm pissed about this."

Gorcoff told them about his experiences with Aunty,

about the notes and the fight we had over the kitchen
sink and about how grumpy she got at night time.
Jesse stopped being mad and became uncharacteristically
sympathetic.

"Grimboli that shit is depressing as hell."

"I know."

"Grimboli..."

"What?"

"I got to see one of those notes."

"No, I can't."

"Why not?"

"I just can't..."

"Grimboli, if you don't go in there and get them, I'll
have to do it for you."

"Jesse, please, don't."

"Grimboli, I'm being really serious right now. I will go
in there."

"Don't," I said, giving in. "I'll go."

As I searched for a note I could hear Aunty sleeping. I
could also hear Harold. They both kept groaning and moving
around restlessly. It was like they were both having the same
bad dream.

I found a few notes, but only one of them was juicy
enough to satisfy Jesse. The other two were boring. One was
about having to get to work early and the other was about a
splinter she had. "Luckily it wasn't too big," it read.

Jesse was mad that I only found one note.

"This better be really fucking good," he said. "I mean I
want to hear some real bleak , sad, psycho old lady shit."

"Don't worry, it's good," I said.

"Then read it, man."

"Ok here we go. It says, 'hi...'"

"Wait," Jesse interrupted. "It starts by saying hi?"

I nodded.

"Do they all start that way?"

"No. Just listen. It says 'hi. I have just recently noticed that I write everything very small. I think this is because I am so insecure.' Now look." I showed them the note. "Look at how small her hand writing is."

"Holy fuck!" Milz said.

Everyone was in complete awe.

Jesse broke the silence.

"You need a fucking magnifying glass to read that shit," he said.

"I know."

Out of nowhere, Slim jumped up and started howling and running at the house. When he got close he stopped and then chucked his cell phone, it explode against the garage door. We all looked down at the pieces of cell phone scattered in my yard, then we looked back up at Slim.

"Are you ok?" I asked.

"Hell yeah," he said. "Obviously. I'm just tired."

Slim stumbled towards the van.

"I'm going to sleep out here," he said.

He crawled under the van. It was like he was trying to use the vehicle as a blanket.

"Slim is nuts," Milz commented. "I'm going to go pass out in the back seat. Fuck it."

Jesse called me over.

"Grimboli," he said. "You and Gorcoff aren't trying to sleep right? Cause I'm trying to go on all night."

"I'm tired," I told him. "But no, I'm not going to go to sleep. I don't think Gorcoff is either."

I looked over at Black Jesse. He had his large hands on Carmen's waist. His fingers dug up her shirt, probing, like the antennae of an insect.

"Look at Black Jesse and Carmen," I said. "Do you think they're going to hook up?"

"Hell naw, watch," Jesse replied.

"Stop touching me!" Carmen yelled. "I don't want to

93

kiss you. I'm friends with your girlfriend. I fucking babysit your children."

Black Jesse looked furious.

"What the fuck you just say? What the fuck you just say?" he yelled. "Why you gotta bring up my kids like that? Why you got to bring up my kids? That's fucked up! Now I know I just a black man living in a white world, I know that shit. I'm just a nigger living in your white ass world, but that don't mean you got to talk about my kids that way!"

"Fuck you, Jesse," Carmen yelled. "I love black guys! I get with black guys all the time!"

Jesse leaned over and started whispering to me.

"Grimboli, we got to get these two out of here or there's going to be a fight."

"What should I do?"

"Drive them home?"

"I can't, Slims under the van. If I move it I'll kill him."

"Then call a cab."

I didn't have much money. Gorcoff could see that I was panicking though and offered to pay.

Luckily, the cab got to the house quickly before Black Jesse and Carmen woke up any of my neighbors and called the cops. We rode with them to ensure they got there separately and by the time we dropped them off, the ride had cost us forty dollars. This made Jesse mad. He spent most of the time driving back berating the driver.

"Look at you!" he said. "Look at that beard! Look at that vest! Did you go to Woodstock, bro?"

"Yes," he said, turning around. "In fact I was present at the original Woodstock."

"Well, fuck you fucking Cherry Garcia and fuck your cab."

The cabby pulled over and kicked us out in the middle of town. We were right in front of the Bagel Buoy, which was just opening.

I rushed into the buoy and ordered two egg and cheese sandwiches, with extra cheese. Jesse ordered the same. Gorcoff got a bagel toasted with butter.

"Who orders a bagel with just butter on it," Jesse said. "You can get that shit at home."

Gorcoff laughed. Then Jesse and I started laughing. We laughed so hard that it seemed like we couldn't stop. What Jesse had said was funny, but not that funny. Still, at this point in the night, anything anyone said was golden.

27

Later that morning I drove Gorcoff to the train station. I was still very drunk. Before he left, Gorcoff pointed out that I had some bagel in my beard. I picked it out flicked it like it was a cigarette, then hugged him and said goodbye.

Aunty was very pleased when she heard that Gorcoff had left.

"I'm just glad to have the house back to normal," she said.

Normal? I thought, what the fuck is normal about this place?

Meanwhile, Harold was barking at the ceiling, his tale was wagging excitedly, like the needle of an old EKG machine. Aunty told me that she thought he was communicating with my mother's ghost.

"What are you talking about?"

"Look at him," she said.

I watched him bark at the ceiling.

"Dog's can't talk," I told her.

"Sure, maybe not the way you or I can, but in his little way he's communicating. Yup, I think he's talking to your mom right now, telling her that we miss her and that we're doing ok...."

The implications of what Aunty was saying were mind shattering. This is what happens when we die? We hide in the corners of rooms and can only communicate through some secret doggy language. Disney would have a field day with this, I thought. Not only would it make a touching movie, but it would also make a great ride. I could imagine kids sitting in cabooses made up to look like giant dogs. Slowly they would be dragged around haunted houses where there were ghosts that walked around barking at you. The kids would all laugh. Ghosts are so silly. Ghosts are so adorable.

I looked up at the corner where Harold was barking. There was a fly up there and it was stuck in a web. I couldn't see any spider. The web looked abandoned. Most likely that is all Harold was barking at.

"Listen," I said to Aunty. "If my mom's up there I would prefer that she talk to me directly. Even if she uses some weird doggy language, even if she's disguised as a dead bug, I would prefer that she talks to me and not some dog."

Aunty looked confused.

"Well, I'm sure she chose Harold to communicate through for a reason."

This made me livid.

"Aunty!" I yelled. "Harold is too dumb to talk to his own asshole! He isn't talking to my mom, he's just barking at a fucking bug!"

Aunty tried not to cry, but the tears gathered up and formed a greasy puddle in her eyes, her lower lip quivered and she clasped her hands together like she was going to pray. Harold turned and walked over to her. He jumped up and put his paws on her lap.

"Well, what do you want?" Aunty asked him. "You want to go outside and go pee pee. Alright, let's go."

She walked Harold outside and I stood there staring at the fly and the web feeling angry.

28

If Harold had a conversation with my mom's ghost, well, he must have really pissed her off, because a week later he was dead.

I expected Aunty to completely fall apart. Instead she just seemed a little more lethargic than usual.

One night she came to my room. I was busy researching episodes of Roseanne. Her lips were tight, trying to hold in the tears.

"How are you doing?" she asked.

"I'm fine," I said.

And then just to cheer her up a bit I lied and told her that I missed the dogs.

"Yup, they were great dogs."

"They sure were," I said.

"We had some good times."

"Sure did."

"And some bad."

"Yup."

"I wouldn't have missed a minute," she said starting to cry again. "I wouldn't have missed a minute of it, not for anything in the world."

I watched her cry. Once she had calmed down and

thoroughly rung out the salt water from her eyes, I invited her to watch Roseanne with me.

She lied on the bed.

"God, she reminds me so much of your mother," she said.

"I know."

After a couple of episodes she fell asleep.

29

The Rugrats started going to a club in Bridgehampton called The O Ring. It was actually just called The Ring, but the graphic of the ring was so simple that it looked like an O. An O ring was what we called condoms. When the club was lame we called it a blown out O ring or just said it was soggy.

It was a fun club, but expensive. I used this as an excuse to stop hanging around the Rugrats. Though the times we had were often fun, they were also exhausting. I started seeing them less and less.

I got a job at the public library. It was easy. All I had to do was fix light bulbs. Kalish was back in town though and we were drinking a lot; I kept sleeping through my shift. After a couple weeks they fired me.

Still, I had some money and decided to blow out the old O ring. Kalish came with.

When we got there we saw Jesse and the rest of them standing out back, passing around a bottle of rum.

"Don't even walk up to us!" he yelled.

I figured he was just joking so I continued approaching and they continued attacking me.

"Look at him and that sweatshirt and those huge tits. Holy shit, he looks like fucking Dolly Parton in that movie

The *Best Little Whore House in Texas.*"

Kalish laughed and then apologized for laughing.
We walked past them, trying to act unfazed. I felt like a little
kid getting bullied on the play ground or a pregnant chick
walking past protestors on the way to the abortion clinic.

When we were inside Kalish got into an argument with
Jesse. He was starting a clothing line and he wanted Kalish
to help. It was going to be called Privileged Design. The first
shirt was going to have a picture of a one dollar bill and a
hundred dollar bill. He needed Kalish to design it so George
Washington was pouting and looking up at the hundred
dollar bill. Underneath it was going to say GREEN WITH
ENVY. Jesse told Kalish his idea and he just laughed.

"It's funny isn't it?" Jesse said. "But it's fucking smart
too."

"I was laughing 'cause of how bad it is," Kalish said.

Jesse came up to me and said we needed to talk.

"Grimboli," he said. "You and Kalish need to get out of
here."

"Why?"

"Cause your boy keeps running his mouth."

"He just didn't like your t-shirt design."

"He was disrespectful. If he sticks around it's going
to get him beat. Grimboli, I know tons of blacks that would
thrash the shit out of both of you if I asked."

"You always sound so silly when you talk about black
people," I said.

"Watch yourself Grimboli!"

He walked away and then I found Kalish. I told him
that I wasn't feeling well and that I wanted to go home. He
seemed relieved to have an excuse to leave.

After picking up some beers at 7-Eleven, we drove
back to my house and spent the night in the garage drinking.

As a joke I told him this elaborate story about how
I had recently robbed a gas station with the Rugrats. He

believed me. I was shocked.

"I can't believe you think that I would rob a gas station," I said.

"Shit, I don't know... you fucking worship those kids."

This got to me. Though I had recently started to discontinue my relationship with them, I found how Kalish was mocking our friendship to be offensive.

I was so upset that I ran at him and tried to tackle him. He was like a brick wall. Though I was much larger than him I was still not nearly as strong.

To punish me for attacking him, Kalish pushed me into the ground.

I started to cry.

He apologized and let me go. I started mumbling about respect and love and my mother and the Rugrats and how they all had everything and nothing to do with each other and in my mind's little heart, I felt like I was making sense, but I could tell by the way Kalish was looking at me that he couldn't understand a word of what I was saying.

We continued drinking and Kalish let me ramble until I wasn't mad anymore and could barely talk. Then we went to bed.

I told Kalish not to drive and he promised he wouldn't, but when I got into bed I heard his car start up and then peel out of my driveway. For the next ten minutes or so I lied awake anxiously until he finally called.

"Sorry," he said. "But you know how much I hate sleep-overs."

"I know," I told him.

Then I hung up and went back to sleep.

30

The sun came in through my window in the morning and it was as beautiful as a hunger pain. My home felt like a litter box and sleep seemed like it should be avoided, like dog shit or AIDS....

I woke up feeling nauseous, stumbled out into the living room and lied down on the couch. I looked around at all the knick-knacks my family had collected over the years. It was hard to believe that we lived in the Hamptons. The house looked more like a bed and breakfast that could be found in the Midwest. I couldn't stand the night clubs anymore, but I also didn't like how hard my home tried to be wholesome. Both places tried to be safe and clean. Neither succeeded. All they did was worsen my hangover.

Sally called and asked if I could watch Samuel.

"You know I love seeing Samuel," I told her, "but every time I do, you are hours late to pick him up."

"I'm sorry," she said. "I won't be late this time, I promise. I'll pick him up at eleven."

"Sally you just told me you were going to be here by ten."

"I know, but then I realized it might be more like eleven."

"Sally, my buddy Kalish is going to be here at ten. I plan on drinking as soon as he arrives. I have no problem with getting hammered in front of children and I want you to know that."

"Fine," she said. "I'll be there at ten."

Kalish showed up at ten thirty carrying two twelve packs of Corona. Samuel was sitting in front of the TV watching *America's Funniest Videos*. He didn't seem very amused.

"Where's his mom?" Kalish asked.

"I don't know."

"Should we start drinking?"

"Sure."

Kalish opened two bottles and then put the rest in the refrigerator. We tried to pace ourselves. This never worked. Whenever we consciously tried to pace ourselves we did the opposite and started drinking at an even more absurd pace than usual.

By eleven o'clock we were fully drunk.

Samuel thought this was hilarious. He liked seeing adults act silly. He especially liked Kalish because of how long and goofy looking his body was. Eventually he started climbing on him and trying to wrestle with him. Kalish hated this. He was a very clean and proper man, while Samuel was wearing nothing but his underpants and smelled like pepperoni.

"Stop!" Kalish begged.

"Oh-you-shuh-up!" Samuel responded, half mumbling. This was one of the few things he knew how to say and he said it as if it was one word.

"Please god! Have mercy!" Kalish yelled.

Samuel laughed and laughed. I loved watching them. Samuel was a genius comedian. He understood the importance of laughter. As long as he laughed the joke was good. It was that simple. There was no need to be clever or witty.

The wrestling made him tired though, and soon he was asleep.

Kalish looked over at me. "Grimboli, is what just happened ok? I feel like I just hooked up. At one point he had his butt against my face. The only time I ever get that close to an asshole is when I'm eating pussy. God, that was truly awful."

"I thought it was wonderful," I said to him.

"Of course you did," he said then he looked down at his hands like they were covered in blood.

Samuel had begun to snore.

"I wonder what he's dreaming about," Kalish said.

"Me too. I hope it's decent though. My dreams are fucked. They're always about my mother, but they're never nice dreams. She's always, like, half retarded or mean."

"Really? You have dreams like that a lot?"

"All the time."

"Shit, Grimboli, that's awful."

The phone rang. It was Sally. She apologized for being late and asked me to pick up her other son Tory, Samuel's older brother. She said she would be there in a half an hour. I agreed, but I reminded her that I was getting drunk.

"The longer you take to get here the drunker I'll get in front of your children," I told her. "Do you understand this? There is no telling what strange shit they will get exposed to!"

"I'll be there soon," she said, then hung up.

Tory was at a party at Long Beach. The place was swarming with teenagers, mainly rich girls with frantic eyes, grouping together like an ant pile and gossiping with the boys and slowly, cautiously, fumbling around the perimeter, hoping to get caught in it all.

Tory stood out from the rest of the boys. Most of

the kids his age still looked like little boys, where he had grown to be a towering six feet tall and was sporting a dark moustache.

As soon as he got in the car he started bragging about his night, about the girl he had just fingered, about how drunk she was and how her tongue was cold and tasted like an orange.

It made me feel nostalgic. I missed being young and sneaking around. I missed the way pussy felt back then. Just touching the pubic hair was exciting enough. Hell, even porn was better. It was hard to come by and when you did find some, well, it made jerking off feel downright intimate.

"Have you guys ever huffed glue?" Tory asked us.

We both told him we had not.

"It's so much fun."

"You probably shouldn't do that stuff," Kalish told him.

"Why? Do you think it's bad for you?"

"Wasn't there a warning label on the container?"

"I don't think so..."

"I'm sure there was," Kalish asserted.

"Well, does that mean it's bad for you?" Tory asked.

"Yes, Tory, it's bad for you."

We got back to my place and Kalish and I continued drinking. Tory tried to sneak drinks, so we decided to play a trick on him. We hid most of the beers outside. Then we pissed in some empty bottles and put the caps back on and put them in the fridge. But I ended up being so drunk, that I forgot about the prank and ended up grabbing one of the piss filled beers.

"Grimboli! What the hell are you doing?" Kalish yelled.

The beer was an inch away from my tiny lips.

At this point Tory was asleep on the floor. He was lying next to his brother and they were both snoring.

Kalish and I decided to leave them with Aunty and go to the Headlights, a bar down town. The Rugrat's had always refused to go there. They said there were too many dads there.

And they were right. There was the same sleazy old men at the Headlights as there was at the stripper party. We also ran into some people we used to go high school with, Robin and Jim. They looked old.

They started reminiscing with us.

"Hey Grimboli, do you remember when we used to call you table butt?" Robin asked.

"You called me that?"

"Sure, everyone did, 'cause you had such a big ass."

"Well that's true."

Kalish laughed then put his hand on my shoulder and apologized. "I'm sorry Grimboli."

I hated when he did that.

"It's fine," I told him, then I walked off to the bar to get a beer.

While I was ordering a man named Rooster approached me. He was compact, angry and red-faced, but it was a natural redness that seemed like it would have been there even if he was calm.

"You're Pastor Chris' son," he told me.

I agreed. I was Pastor Chris' son. Her death had been taunting me, making me an emotional water balloon for the past six years. I was tired of it. Even hearing old nick-names I had in middle school made me want to cry.

"I was in her youth group in '84. Do you remember me?" he asked.

"No," I told him. "I was only two years old then."

"My name is Rooster," he said.

"I know," I said.

"Do you know Charley, my brother?"

"No," I said.

He looked at me hard for a short, but uncomfortable length of time.

"Your mother was a good fucking woman," he told me.

"I know," I said. "She was wonderful."

He looked upset with me. I couldn't understand why.

"I have to go to the bathroom," he said.

He went to the bathroom and stayed there for at least twenty minutes. When he came out his eyes looked desperate and sad, but not angry.

"I need another bag," he said to me.

"Of what?" I asked.

"What the fuck do you think, porky?"

"I really have no idea what you are talking about."

"I need another bag."

"Of what?" I asked.

"Blow, big man, I need that yayo, cocaine, you hear me... I was in the bathroom takin' a dump when I dropped my bag in the toilet. It was really upsetting, man. I hit the wall and hurt my knuckles. Come on, give me another bag. I got 60 bucks. Here take it."

He held out a ball of sweaty money. I could have really used the money.

"I don't have any cocaine," I told him.

He looked at me with the same anger he had when he told me my mother was a good woman. A sort of old, senile anger. Nursing home anger. The type of anger men get when they are too drunk.

Rooster walked away from me and started badgering another man about the cocaine. This man seemed used to him though. He didn't seem as confused as I had been. He put his arm around him and whispered jokes in his ear. Rooster seemed calmed. I would like to think I could do that for old friends just as easily. One can only hope to be on the other side of the dynamic, to be the supportive buddy and not Rooster.

I walked up to the bar and took a seat next to a young woman. She had dark hair and eyes, and cheeks that were chubby like a new born baby.

She was typing something into her cell phone.

"That's a really fancy cell phone," I said to her awkwardly.

She smiled at me then continued typing.

"I'm amazed with how futuristic things have gotten," I said.

"What do you mean?" she asked.

"Your cell phone, it's the type of shit we used to see in science fiction movies, you know?"

"I never watched those kinds of movies," she said.

"Of course not," I said. "But it's still VERY impressive. I mean we got five year olds surfing the net on their cell phones while riding the bus to school. While we used to pass notes in class, they check emails and look at porn."

"It is kind of strange," she admitted.

"I personally can't wait to see what they come up with next," I said.

"I'm sure you can't."

"I'll tell you what I want, I want them to create a cure for hangovers. A real cure. Not that bullshit you can get at 7-Eleven."

"I already invented that," she said.

"How?" I asked.

"Just don't drink," she said.

"That's silly," I said. "It's like trying to cure pregnancy by not having sex."

"I don't think it's silly at all," she said and then got back to typing into her cell phone.

I noticed that she was drinking water. She was probably just waiting to drive a friend home. She was sober and I wanted nothing to do with that sort of behavior.

Instead of attempting to talk to her more, I grabbed my beer and rejoined Rooster, who was sitting at the other end of the bar, staring at his drink and chewing his own teeth. He had definitely found some cocaine. It made my jaw hurt just too look at him.

He began to tell me about a friend of his who died.

"His name was Theo and he accidentally shot himself. Do you remember him?"

"Yes," I said. "I do."

I was three when Theo died, but my mother had told me about him many times, about how he killed himself and how it hurt his friends and how they all turned into drunks. I think she told me about Theo Goldbrook so often, as a way to remind me of how fragile we are when it comes to death.

"Your mom was so fat," he said. "And funny too. I had never known a woman minister let alone one that was so fat and so funny and seriously, after my buddy died I got so upset and depressed that I wouldn't get out of bed. One time I was in that bed for days. I swear to god. And then one day your mom comes in my room and gets into bed with me and tells me that she wasn't going to get out of my bed unless I did. So I started to laugh like a crazed bastard because, shit, I had this fat lady minister in my fucking bed with me and what's not funny about that.

"Seriously though, it was the first time I had laughed in long time, man. She was a good woman. She got me out of bed and she got me laughing and she got me feeling a little less awful and it's rare that a woman will do that for you. You know what I mean?"

I didn't say much. It was all true. My mother had good comedic timing and a large soft body. She was very comforting. She also cried a lot. And when she cried she sounded like a child. I'm sure Rooster had no idea how often that woman cried.

"I'm sorry I called your mom fat," he told me.

"It's fine," I said.

He looked angry again.

"Listen," he said. "I'm sorry I called your mom fat. She was a good lady."

"It's fine," I said.

"I'm sorry," he said.

Kalish and I got home and found Tory in the garage sitting on the broken down La-Z-Boy, talking on his cell phone.

"You're aunt seemed really mad," Tory told me. "She started ranting about how she was going to have to sleep in the basement. I felt really bad."

"Don't. It's well furnished. Her bedroom's down there."

He looked confused.

"She normally sleeps on the couch."

"So should I feel bad?" he asked, still feeling confused.

"No."

"Who were you just talking to?" I asked.

"That was just a girl."

"What's her name?"

"Lina."

As soon as Kalish realized we were talking about girls he became crazed.

"You give that girl the sledgehammer," he told Tory. "You hear me! You don't let that little minnow swim away. You tell her about the big bang and how the biggest bang comes from your ding-dong!"

Tory laughed uncomfortably. "I don't understand what you are talking about."

"I'm telling you to man up!" Kalish yelled. "Stop just fingering your own dick hole and get that girl, Lemo or Lono or whatever the fuck you call her and you give her some power saw. Say to her, 'Listen, I'm pure rampage.' You tell her that."

I explained to Tory that Kalish had gotten his heart broken a few years back and that it hadn't healed right, so now, when he moves it in certain directions it hurts and he starts to act sad in a way that comes across as crazy.

"Listen," Kalish added. "I have been to the doctors many times. I have had x-rays taken and they have told me that my DNA is endlessly, well, complicated. You see, while most DNA has an A-C-T-G nucleo-basis, mine has K-A-L-I-S-H. They told me that the Kalish heart is broken, but that it doesn't matter 'cause my brain power is so intense that it teaches the blood how to pump itself."

"Why is he talking about DNA?" Tory asked.

I didn't answer.

"I need sleep," Kalish said. "I need dreamland. Even though nothing's very happy there either."

I went outside and smoked a cigarette with Tory and then I went to sleep. As I lied in bed I could hear Tory slowly sneak into the basement to grab a beer.

31

When I woke up in the morning I found Samuel and my aunt in the living room watching TV. Tory and Kalish were still asleep on the floor.

"Samuel's watching my Soaps with me," Aunty said.

I sat on the couch next to them and watched the Soap. It was bad. Very complicated. I couldn't tell what was going on. Everyone seemed very attractive and very upset.

Aunty knew exactly what was going on. She had been watching this show for years.

"How long has this show been on for?" I asked.

"Oh, I would say a half hour or so..."

"No, I mean, how many years, how many seasons has it been aired for?"

"About thirty I think."

"Really? Thirty years? And is it all connected? Does each episode run into the next?"

"Sure," she said.

"Are there still characters left over from the first season?"

"Of course! You see that girl, well, she was born in the first season and sometimes her parents come back as ghosts. And you see the black doctor, the really handsome one, well, he was been on the show from the beginning as well."

I was amazed. The whole thing seemed so epic. It didn't matter how horribly written it was or how bad the acting was. The show had been going on for thirty years. People like my aunt had gotten attached to it. She probably hadn't questioned whether the show was good or not. It didn't matter. Quality, finally, meant very

little. All that mattered was that it had managed to be in her life for a long, long time.

Kalish got up briefly and tried to watch the show with us.

"What is this?" he asked.

"It's a soap opera," I told him.

"I hate it," he groaned.

He then buried his face in the couch pillow and went back to sleep.

"Well, isn't he just Mister Chipper," Aunty said.

I looked over at Samuel. He seemed very content.

"Hey Samuel, what do you think of this show?" I asked.

He didn't reply. He just laughed and then stuck his finger in my ear.

Also Available From Black Coffee Press

www.blackcoffeepress.net

Putting the "F" back in Fiction.

CPSIA information can be obtained at www.ICGtesting.com

264542BV00001B/13/P